Shake the Trees

Gregory Payette

8 Flags Publishing

Copyright © 2021 by Gregory Payette

8 Flags Publishing

Print ISBN: 978-1-7361465-7-6

All rights reserved.

This book is licensed for your personal enjoyment only. All rights reserved. This is a work of fiction. All characters and events portrayed in this book are fictional, and any resemblance to real people or incidents is purely coincidental. This book, or parts thereof, may not be reproduced in any form without permission in writing from the publisher or author, except as permitted by U.S. copyright law.

Chapter 1

Frank didn't look up when Charlie walked into his office. He just sat there, sipping his coffee as if Charlie wasn't there, reading whatever was inside the manila folder he had in front of him. It must've been at least a minute or two, or at least felt that way, before Frank—still not looking up—wagged his finger for Charlie to close the door. "Have a seat," he said, then pulled his reading glasses from his face and placed them on his desk.

Charlie gently closed the door and stood there, waiting. He cleared his throat.

Chief Deputy Carter finally raised his gaze from the documents on his desk to Charlie. "Did it ever cross your mind there might've been a second suspect?"

Charlie sat down in one of two cracked leather chairs across from Frank. "Of course it did, Frank. Who do you think we've been doing all afternoon? Between me and Kim, and I'd say at least a dozen deputies from the sheriff's office, we knocked on every door—over seventy-five mobile homes in that park, and—"

"I'm not asking if you looked for him *after the fact*, Charlie. You don't think I know that?" Frank squinted his eyes and leaned forward, his elbows down on the desk. He folded his hands together, held them up under his chin. He looked down at the paper and picked it up, reading it over. "You shot Gunner King dead. Yet we have no way of knowing he's the man who pulled that trigger. And if we can't confirm he's the man who killed Teddy, then—"

"Come on, Frank. You think I'm making up a story here? That he fired at me? Only missed me by a few inches. What was I really supposed to do? Run and hide?" He held his gaze on Frank.

"Gunner didn't have a gun," Frank said. "Not when deputies got to him."

The door opened behind Charlie and he turned to look.

Deputy Kim Riggins stepped in and sat in the chair to Charlie's right.

Frank had his eyes on her. "Any luck?"

Kim shook her head. "According to descriptions provided by witnesses—at least the ones willing to talk—it sure does sound like it was the older brother, Hunter. He must've gotten out ahead of Gunner before Charlie got back there, maybe ran in another direction entirely." She gave Charlie a quick glance from the corner of her eye but held her gaze on Frank. "It doesn't mean Gunner didn't pull the trigger."

Charlie leaned forward on the chair, his elbows on his thighs as he rubbed his face with one hand. He said to Frank, "Don't you think we oughta be out there right now, looking for Hunter?"

Frank took a deep breath and sighed, cleared his throat as he leaned back in his brown leather chair. He glanced at Kim, then shifted his eyes to Charlie. "You know what I'm scared of right now?" He nodded at the phone on the desk in front of him. "I'm scared that phone's gonna ring any minute, and Director Lang or, shit, the US Attorney General herself's gonna be on the other end to give me an earful of—"

"Frank, let's be honest here," Charlie said. "Before we get our panties all bunched up. The truth is we went to serve a warrant, and nobody answered the door. So we let ourselves in and next thing you know Ted Moore's crumpled on the ground, got a hole in his chest. I went after the suspect and did what I had to do to—"

"You shot a man, Charlie. That's twice in six months. And the question going to be raised is how the hell could you identify the suspect from fifty yards away? Gunner doesn't look any different than—"

"I'd actually say it was closer to a hundred yards," Charlie said. He gave Kim a quick look out of the corner of his eye, a slight smirk on his face he knew Frank wouldn't appreciate.

"Christ, Charlie. You even try to run after him? Or you lick those lips of yours and take aim, like it's all a goddamn game..."

Charlie leaned back in the chair and put one leg up, his ankle rested across the top of his knee. He picked a small stone from the bottom of his boot and rolled it between his fingers.

Frank raised his voice and said to Charlie, "You think this is a joke?" He turned his eyes toward Kim. "And can you please tell me one more time why you weren't there? If not to help him, then to at least babysit the man, keep him out of trouble like I've asked you to?"

Charlie looked at her, watched her swallow and gather her thoughts. "I was late, sir. Told Deputy Harlow to go ahead without me. I was supposed to meet him there sooner than the time I arrived, but—"

"Now wait a minute," Charlie said. He straightened out in the chair. "Don't believe a word she's telling you." He shook his head. "She wasn't late at all. *We* were early. Me and Teddy and the other deputy, whatever the kid's name is... agreed it'd be a piece of cake for the three of us."

Frank stared back at Charlie, his eyelids heavy. "Didn't turn out to be a piece of cake, now did it."

SHAKE THE TREES

Charlie looked to his right, at Kim. "I appreciate you trying to cover my ass, but no sense in both of us being hung out by our drawers for how this went down."

Charlie sat alone at the dimly lit bar inside the Coyote Grille, a glass of whiskey in his hand resting on the bar. He stared straight ahead, music playing from the jukebox in the background. He looked up and tried to catch what they were saying on the news, his own picture in a superimposed box over the shoulder of the newsman on the screen.

The place brightened up a bit when the door behind him opened and Frank walked in. He sat on the stool to Charlie's left and held his finger up to the pretty bartender.

She poured a glass of Jack Daniels and placed it down in front of him. "Good afternoon, Frank," she said.

He nodded. "Thanks, Lindsey."

Charlie kept his eyes on the TV, shot back what was left in his glass and slid it forward on the bar. "I'll have one more." He pointed with his thumb at Frank. "And put his on my tab."

Charlie and Frank both watched Lindsey grab Charlie's glass and walk the other way in her skintight blue jeans.

Frank held his glass in front of his mouth. "I'll do whatever I can to protect you, Charlie. But you've gotten yourself a reputation now."

Lindsey filled Charlie's glass and slid it in front of Charlie, gave him a look Frank must've noticed because he looked back and forth between the two until Charlie turned to him and grinned, sipping his whiskey.

Frank held his gaze for a moment, shaking his head. "Right now," he said, "we're going to let the police do their job, do their investigation and follow all the proper channels."

Charlie turned in his seat, his right elbow up on the bar. "But if Hunter was there with Gunner and there's a chance he's the one who killed Ted... and tried to take me out, then wouldn't I help find him?"

Frank sipped his Jack. "Well, we don't know if it was Hunter or not. And now some of those witnesses who claimed to've seen another man run from the back of that home aren't so sure what they saw, whether it was Hunter or someone else."

"Maybe he got to some of them?" Charlie said.

Frank shrugged, sipping his drink. "Maybe." He looked around the bar, turned back to Charlie. "I know you don't want to hear this, but if Gunner was alive..."

Charlie kept his gaze on Frank and ran his tongue inside his cheek, Frank looking straight ahead with the glass held up in front of him. Charlie said, "Well, if Ted Moore'd still been alive…"

Frank cleared his throat and shot back what was left in his glass. "There'll be an internal review. You know that already. The state bureau'll be involved, of course." He pushed his glass forward on the bar. "Lindsey? Just one more." He turned to Charlie. "You know what that means, don't you?"

Charlie nodded. "It means you gotta get me another assignment right away before I'm stuck sitting at a desk for the next six months."

Frank had a manilla folder next to him on his left, picked it up and dropped it on the bar between him and Charlie. "I knew you were going to say that."

Lindsey poured another strong shot of Jack Daniels into Frank's empty glass.

Frank said to Charlie, "You and Kim'll have to go down to Monroe. You know where that is? Just south of Charlotte?"

Charlie nodded. "Yes, of course I do. What's it about?" He had the folder opened and skimmed over the papers tucked inside.

"Man's name is Jack Thornton. Posted bail and disappeared. It's believed he's shacked up with his young girlfriend on her family's farm."

"What'd he do?"

"White-collar. Stole a lot of money from a lot of people. I don't believe he's dangerous, but you never know with some of these guys, the way they'll fight to the death to hang on to their money."

Charlie flipped through the pages in the folder. "I'll study up." He closed the folder and picked up his drink. "Just me and Kim?"

Frank nodded. "Yes, and she's the lead on this one."

Charlie gave Frank a look from the corner of his eye, finished his glass and stood up from the stool. "Take me a half day. You got anything else when I'm done, let me know. You know I don't like to sit around."

"Not just yet," he said. "But don't worry, there'll be plenty of paperwork waiting for you when you get back. Someone from the bureau will be coming to interview you. Just be straight with whoever it is shows up... we can hopefully move past this and get back to work."

Charlie pulled cash from his pocket and threw it up on the bar, giving Lindsey a nod. He turned to Frank, "Doesn't it matter to anyone an officer of the law's been shot?"

Frank kept his gaze straight ahead, his glass up to his mouth. "Maybe if it'd been your first time."

Chapter 2

Kim was behind the wheel of the black Chevy Tahoe, Charlie in the passenger seat with his foot up on the dash. He had his eyes out the passenger window to his right, neither saying much at all.

Kim had the radio on, music Charlie wasn't familiar with and didn't like very much. She was younger than him by a handful of years and their taste in music didn't exactly jive.

"I can handle this one alone," Charlie said. "If you want to just wait in the car, it shouldn't be much of—"

"Frank does *not* want you doing *anything* on your own right now." She gave him a quick glance from the driver's seat. "So, no, you're not even walking to that door by yourself. And you might want to get used to me being stuck to you even more than before. Like Velcro."

Charlie smiled, kept his eyes on her for a moment, then turned back to the passenger window. He watched the mountains along East I-40, puffy white clouds hanging over them so you couldn't see the peaks. He picked up the folder between the seats and opened it. Jack Thornton's picture was attached to the first page with a paperclip. "I hope I look this good when I'm sixty-five," he said.

Kim said, "Some of the money he stole from his clients went to plastic surgery."

Charlie looked up from the folder. "No shit?"

"Didn't you read the reports?" she said.

"I'm reading right now."

"The girlfriend has horses, some he allegedly purchased for her. I bet she's going to be pretty upset when they're taken away."

Charlie turned and looked into the back seat over his shoulder. "You sure they're going to fit back there?"

Kim gave him a look, rolling her eyes. "Trailers'll be there tomorrow. Got eleven of them."

Charlie flipped through the papers he hadn't exactly studied before the trip like he said he would. "She's twenty-nine?" he said.

"The girlfriend?" Kim nodded and glanced at the photo in Charlie's hand. "Former Miss Union County."

He studied the eight-by-ten photo of the attractive blonde; didn't look a day over twenty-two. "They're really buying she didn't know a thing about what he was up to?" Charlie said.

"Well, she knows now," Kim said. "But he's still down there with her on her farm, like the good times'll just keep rolling for them."

"So it's *her* farm? How's that?"

"Her family owns it. She grew up in the house. Forty-seven acres."

"Gotta be worth quite a bit of money," Charlie said.

Kim still had her eyes ahead on the road, nodding her head.

Charlie had fallen asleep and had just started to wake up, rolling his head against the headrest to watch Kim turn the steering wheel heading off Route 74 and into Monroe.

They drove another two miles and turned when the female voice on the GPS on Kim's phone told them to.

Charlie straightened up in the passenger seat. "You sure this is it?"

Kim didn't answer. They stopped at the faded red mailbox shaped like a barn, with the name *Ray* painted on the side, the letters chipped and faded.

She turned down the dirt driveway and drove a good hundred yards, stopping behind a silver Audi parked beside a red, new-looking pickup truck.

Charlie removed his hat from his head and brushed his hand over the six-pointed star stitched to the front, placed it down on the console between the seats. He nodded toward the red truck. "I wouldn't mind a nice pickup like that," he said. "Although I don't know how much I like the red." He cracked a small smile and turned to Kim, a slight tilt to his head. "They say red vehicles get pulled over more. But it's actually white vehicles that get the most tickets." He pushed open the door and stepped down onto the dirt.

Kim walked around to him from the other side. She said, "They'll take the Audi tomorrow when they come for the horses. I didn't see anything about a red truck being seized."

Charlie stood behind the Audi and looked it over. "Maybe I'll save 'em a trip, take it back myself." He walked ahead of Kim toward the two-story farmhouse with yellow wood siding and black shutters on the windows. He stopped at the bottom of the steps leading to the covered porch. Two rocking chairs were placed on either side of the front door.

He didn't see any horses, but thought he heard one of them neigh.

He walked up the steps ahead of Kim and onto the porch, turned and glanced back at her and took a good look around at all the open land and the tall grass in the field. The property was surrounded by woods and lots of pine trees.

He stood in front of the door, pushed his hair from his forehead, and glanced one more time over his shoulder at Kim. "You want to go around back?"

She nodded, stepped off the porch and along the grass in front of the house. Her hand was on her Glock 40 but she kept it holstered.

Charlie waited until she turned the corner and gave her a few more seconds to get into position. He knocked on the white wooden frame of the screen door, turned his good ear to the house to listen. But it was quiet. Too quiet. He looked at his watch and gave it another eight seconds, then pulled open the screen door and knocked on the red interior door. He knocked harder this time—and made sure the sound of his knuckles against the wood door wouldn't be missed.

"Mr. Jack Thornton," he said, his voice raised. "This is Deputy U.S. Marshal Charlie Harlow. I've got a warrant for your arrest right here in my hand, and I'd appreciate it if you'd step outside this house without incident. We know you're in there."

"May I help you?" a female voice said from behind him.

Charlie turned, looked down at a pretty young woman with dirty-blonde hair underneath an Atlanta Braves baseball cap. She stood at the bottom of the stairs looking up at him, a pretty smile on her face. She wore cowboy boots and blue jeans, with nothing but a yellow tank top above to show off her tan shoulders.

She had work gloves on her hands and was leaning, holding on to the handle of a spade shovel she'd stuck in the ground in front of her.

Charlie pulled his jacket aside so she could see the badge on his belt. "You must be Bella Ray Sparrow?" he said. "I'm Deputy Marshal Charlie Harlow." He squinted. "Where's your boyfriend?"

Bella Ray pulled off one of her gloves and reached up to shake Charlie's hand as he walked down the stairs. "Sounds like you already know my name. But it's nice to meet you, Deputy." She looked him in the eyes.

Charlie stood in front of her, his eyes moving around the front of the house. "Would you mind telling Mr. Thornton we're waiting for him? I'd prefer it if we didn't have to play any games."

She stared back at Charlie without saying a word.

Charlie held out the warrant. "This here's the warrant for his arrest. If for some reason you'd like to withhold information about his whereabouts, we have room for two in the back of that Tahoe."

Bella Ray shrugged. "I don't know where you get your information, Deputy, but..." She cracked a slight smile, one Charlie thought was cute but could see right through. "Is that what I should call you? Deputy? Or do I call you *Deputy Marshal*? Or are people supposed to use the whole thing? Deputy U.S. Marshal Charlie Harlow..."

Charlie glanced toward the corner of the house where Kim had gone, knowing Bella Ray was playing some kind of game with him.

He didn't like it, whatever it was.

"Ma'am," Charlie said. "We can do this the easy way, or we can do it the hard way. And I'll be honest. I don't mind doing it the hard way at all, but I'd like to give you a choice one more time. But I can promise you, no matter what you're trying to pull, we're not leaving here without Jack Thornton."

Bella Ray turned her head and looked in the direction of the barn, almost the size of the house but up toward the woods a good one hundred yards to the left from the edge of the house.

"Is that where he is?" Charlie said. "Is he hiding in that barn?" Charlie pulled his Glock and started to walk in that direction. But he stopped when Kim came around from the side of the house where he was headed, her hands in the air in front of her.

A man with oddly stretched skin on his face and shoe-polish-black hair that didn't match his aging eyes walked behind her. He had a shotgun pointed at Kim's back.

"Jack?" Bella Ray said, almost believable in how surprised she sounded. "What are *you* doing here?"

Charlie gave her a look, rolling his eyes. "You can cut the act," he said. He glanced at Kim and saw the calm on her face. He shifted his eyes to Jack. "Now, Mr. Thornton, I'd like to make you aware that this in my hand is the warrant for your arrest. And what you're doing there, pointing that rifle there at a law enforcement official and fellow U.S. Marshal is not something I would advise." Charlie folded the paper and tucked it inside his shirt pocket. He removed the Glock from his holster but kept it down by his side.

Thornton was shorter than Charlie had expected. A good few inches shorter than Kim who was a couple of inches short of six feet. He looked to be heavier than the one-fifty stated in the report. Had to've been close to two hundred, Charlie guessed, with the way his stomach hung over his dress pants and the fat he carried under his chin.

Bella Ray must've fed him well since his initial arrest.

"I'm sorry," Jack said.

Charlie saw the sweat pour from the man's head. He took a step close enough to believe the man wore a toupee. "Put the gun down, Jack." He took a quick glance over his shoulder at Bella Ray, made sure she was still standing in the same spot, not about to pull a fast one to help out her man.

Jack pleaded, "I can't go to jail. I'm sorry for what I did to all those people. But it wasn't just me. I wasn't the only one. Why should I be the only one to pay for it?"

Charlie shrugged. "I'm not the judge or the jury, Jack. I'm just here to do a job and bring you in. And that's what

I intend to do." He looked into Kim's eyes. "Now, why don't you put the gun down, Jack."

Jack Thornton shook his head.

Charlie said, "Here's the story, Jack. You may shoot Deputy Riggins. But if you do, I'm going to shoot you. So we don't really have a whole lot to gain here now, do we?"

"I'd rather die than spend the next thirty years in jail."

Charlie looked at Kim, trying to reassure her he had things under control. "Thirty? Is that what it is?" He shook his head, his lower lip pushed out, the sides of his mouth turned down. "Nah, you go in, do some time, I'd bet you're looking at less than ten on account a good behavior." He shifted his stance, fixing the grip he had on his Glock. "Now, what you're doing there is by no means going to help your cause. Like I said, you're not going to walk away from here without me dragging you back to where you belong. And I'm not sure I care if I have to do it by your arm or your foot, if you know what I mean?"

Charlie looked back at Bella Ray.

She held her gaze on him for a moment, then shifted her eyes to Jack. "Jack, honey. It's over. You don't need to hurt anyone else."

"Anyone else?" Charlie said, his head cocked looking from Bella Ray to Jack. "Uh-oh."

"I don't mean it like that," Bella Ray said. "I mean all those people, lost all that money. That's all I meant."

Charlie nodded, understanding what she meant. "Listen to her, Jack. It's best for everyone." He shifted his stance and raised the Glock. "Now, I'm going to count to three. How's that sound?"

Jack had the barrel of the shotgun shoved into Kim's back with one hand, gripping her arm with the other. He nodded toward the Audi. "Me and the lady are getting in that car. Let's go. Keys are in the ignition."

Kim's calm appearance had changed. She had the look of pain on her face, likely because of the way Jack had pushed the muzzle into her spine. She said, "Charlie, go ahead and take a shot if you got one. I'm okay."

Charlie stood still, watching Jack move toward the Audi, using Kim to shield himself.

Charlie didn't have a shot.

He followed Jack and Kim but looked at the dirt and saw a shadow coming up from behind him. He turned to Bella Ray but it was too late. She'd already come down hard with the spade shovel, brought it down on top of him and caught him right on his head, knocking him down to one knee.

Charlie felt the warmth of his own blood drip through his hair and tried to focus on Kim. But he was seeing two of her. And two of Jack. He hadn't dropped the Glock but couldn't get his hand to move the way he wanted to. He dropped to his side, down into the dry and dusty dirt under him.

Bella Ray stood over him, her long shadow covering his face. "I'm sorry."

Charlie heard the Audi's engine and lifted his head, seeing Jack in the passenger seat and the shotgun on Kim who was now behind the wheel.

Bella Ray lifted the shovel, about to take another good swing at Charlie, do him in for good.

But Charlie reached up and grabbed the wooden handle, caught it just above the steel as she started to come down with it. He ripped it from her hands, using it to push himself to his feet. He turned his Glock on Bella Ray and tossed the shovel far out of her reach. His head was both pounding and burning at the same time. "Get down on the ground and put your hands behind your head where I can see them." He stood up and straddled over her, had the handcuffs off his belt and onto her wrists in one motion before she spoke another word.

Chapter 3

Charlie looked up in the rearview at Bella Ray, handcuffed in the back seat of Kim's Tahoe. She certainly didn't look the type to knock a federal law enforcement official in the back of the head with a shovel. But she sure as hell did it and, as far as Charlie was concerned, she was going to pay for her mistake. Although he was more worried at that point about finding Kim.

"If he hurts her, Bella Ray, I promise you I'll—"

"He won't. He doesn't hurt people. Not like that."

"Then tell me where they could've gone," he said, his eyes in the rearview.

"I swear to you, I don't know where they were going," she said. "I think he was just surprised you were there, caught him off guard. He said nobody'd come for him until sometime this afternoon. He hadn't planned to run like that."

Charlie had the Tahoe moving at a pretty good clip, the speedometer at ninety, heading southeast on 74 toward

601. He'd done nothing more than guessed they must've headed in that direction.

He called Frank to tell him Jack Thornton had escaped. "He's got Kim with him... driving his car. I was hoping he would've let her off someone on the road, but it's not looking that way so far."

"Jesus Christ, Charlie. How the hell'd you let this happen?"

Charlie didn't answer, knowing Frank didn't always think first before he spoke. He glanced up in the rearview. "I've got the girlfriend in the back, handcuffed to the door."

"You call the locals?"

"Not yet. Thought you could maybe get an air unit out here. They have choppers in Charlotte, don't they?"

"CMPD does, yes."

"I'm in Union County, heading in the other direction."

"I'll call the sheriff's office over there," Frank said, and hung up the phone.

Charlie kept his eyes on the road, glanced back over his shoulder and said to Bella Ray, "You cooperate, maybe I can get that home run swing you took to my head swept under the rug. One way or another, your boyfriend's going to jail. Might as well tell me where you think they could be heading and maybe you won't have to join him."

Bella Ray sat quiet for a moment. "I'm not sure," she said. "But I know he's got a friend with a plane."

Charlie had his eyes in the rearview. "What airport?"

"Monroe Executive."

"Aw, shit," Charlie said, slammed on the brakes and cut the wheel, took the Tahoe across the grass median, both Charlie and Bella Ray bouncing in their seats, and hit the asphalt on 74 going northwest to where Charlie had seen the signs for the local airport.

"Please don't tell him I told you," she said.

Charlie didn't respond, stuck his chin over the steering wheel so he could see a little higher in the sky through the top of the windshield. He thought he'd heard a helicopter, but didn't see one. He couldn't imagine CMPD could get theirs out there that fast, but maybe they were somehow already in the area. He hoped so.

Even if Jack Thornton got off the ground, it was likely a puddle jumper. Maybe a small jet.

"Is Jack a licensed pilot?" Charlie said.

Bella Ray paused a moment. "His ex-wife is."

"Ex-wife? Is it her plane?"

"Sort of. His friend owns it. I think Jack paid for it, but..."

"Hiding his assets," Charlie said. "This friend of his got a name?" he turned to look back at Bella Ray.

She nodded. "Roger Flynn."

"And what about this wife of his, is she—"

"Ex-wife," Bella Ray said.

"Okay, ex-wife. Minor detail. She got a name?"

Bella Ray paused again before she answered, but Charlie knew she didn't want to be in the predicament she found herself caught up in. "Elizabeth. She goes by Liz."

"Last name's Thornton?"

"Uh-huh."

Charlie spotted a sign for the airport: *One mile ahead*. "So even if he didn't think we'd be there this morning, he certainly knew we were coming. Had this escape planned out ahead."

Bella Ray didn't respond.

"So where's he going? Mexico? Down Florida? Can't imagine he'd go somewhere up north, right? Man his age ain't going north. Too cold for those old bones of his."

Bella Ray remained quiet.

Charlie's phone rang when he turned the wheel toward the airport's entrance. He looked at the screen and saw it was Frank. He answered, "Got anything?"

"Yeah, CMPD's airborne already, but copter's north of the city. They'll need some time."

"I'm pulling into the airport now, down here in Monroe. My passenger won't say where he's going, but admitted Jack's got a friend with a private plane. He's likely using it to get out of here. I sure as hell hope he doesn't take off, but right now all I'm interested in is knowing Kim's all right."

"I'll get CMPD back on the line, let them know the situation."

Charlie hung up and stopped at a line of orange traffic cones where a Monroe Police officer stood in the middle of Paul J. Helms Drive, directing traffic away from the airport's entrance. Charlie put down the window and heard the sirens growing louder from off in the distance. He showed the officer his badge. "Officer, I'm Deputy U.S. Marshal Charlie Harlow. Got a situation in that airport where—"

"I'm real sorry, Deputy. Got a fire inside the building and a possible bomb. We gotta move all vehicles out of the area."

Charlie could see the entrance from where he was stopped. The airport was only one level, made of brick. He didn't see any signs about departure or arrivals except two separate doors on the front of the building.

"Right, well I've got a fugitive possibly about to take off on one of those planes. He's got a deputy U.S. Marshal held captive."

The tall officer ducked down and looked into the back seat at Bella Ray, then straightened out and glanced toward the airport.

"She's my prisoner," Charlie said. He gave the officer a nod. "What's my fastest way back there, to the tarmac, without going through the building?"

The officer shook his head. "There's nobody inside. The building's cleared out. Bomb Squad from Charlotte

Mecklenburg PD's en route right now. I'm sorry, but I can't let you back there."

The sirens grew louder and Charlie turned to see two fire engines driving toward them.

"I understand you're doing your job, officer. But I am a federal marshal." He looked at the building and at the surrounding area. He could see a handful of parked planes. "You notice there's no smoke or flame anywhere over there?"

The officer looked at the building.

"I'm willing to bet her life," Charlie said, his thumb pointed over his shoulder at Bella Ray, "that her boyfriend, the man I'm after, has created this diversion with one simple phone call. And I'm willing to take a chance."

The officer looked back and forth and pointed toward a road fifty yards from where they stood. "Turn down that road over there; you'll be able to park your car at the other side of the airport. You'll see a gate. TSA agents have cleared everyone out. But the gate's still open."

Charlie said thank you, tipped his hat to the officer and drove away. He parked just outside the open gate and took Bella Ray around to the front seat on the driver's side, cuffed her to the steering wheel.

He closed the door and locked her inside, looked up when he heard a jet fly overhead before they even made it to the entrance. "Shit," he said, wondering if Jack had already escaped. He picked up the pace and started to run.

He made it through the gate and stopped when he heard his name called as he ran past one of the hangars.

He turned to look where it was coming from.

"Charlie!"

He ran into the hangar and saw Kim on the concrete floor, tied with rope to the wheel of a small plane with the door to the engine open.

He crouched down next to Kim. "Where'd he go?"

"I don't know," she said.

Charlie pulled his knife from his belt and cut Kim free. He helped her to her feet. "I'm just happy you're okay."

Kim rubbed her wrists. "He took my gun."

Charlie heard her but his gaze was outside the hangar, seeing the parked planes out on the tarmac. He looked around inside the hangar then walked back outside

Kim followed him. "He called in the bomb scare from the car."

"Figured so," Charlie said. He walked along the back of the building and stopped at a door with OFFICE painted on the glass. He pulled on the knob and walked inside the empty office. There was a damp odor, dark-brown paneling on the walls. The green carpet on the floor was dirty and stained.

"Everybody's been evacuated," Kim said.

Charlie turned to her. "What'd they, run right past you? Leave you there, running for their lives?"

She shook her head. "Nobody saw me. I yelled when I saw a man running by, but he must not've heard me."

"His ex-wife's a pilot," Charlie said.

Kim nodded. "I know."

"How'd you know?" Charlie said.

"I thought you said you read the report?"

Charlie stepped behind one of two desks and leaned down, put his hand on the computer's mouse. The dark screen turned bright blue and his eyes moved around the desktop. A window popped up to sign on. He turned and looked at Kim over his shoulder. "You wanna come over here, see if you can get on this thing?" Charlie knew his way around a computer, but he liked it better without them. Kim was a different story, coming over in a transfer from the Criminal Intelligence Branch to work in the field. She'd spent the early days of her career behind a desk with four monitors in front of her, a large screen up on the wall.

He stepped out of her way.

"It's password protected," she said. She shuffled the papers around on the desk, pulled open the drawers, one at a time, and looked inside. There was a notebook in the drawer on the right; she opened it, and right there on the first page was a row of random letters and numbers. She typed them into the space on the computer. "Never mind," she said. "Got it."

Charlie fixed his hat and looked out the office window to the left of the door toward the two planes on the tarmac. He pulled his phone from his pocket and dialed Frank.

Frank answered on the first ring.

"Kim's right here with me," Charlie said.

"She all right?"

"Yeah, she is." He glanced at Kim. "It's a good possibility the ex-wife is piloting the plane. I assume you read the report as thoroughly as I did," Charlie said. "She's mentioned in there. Mrs. Elizabeth Thornton."

He had his eyes on Kim, waiting.

She looked back at him over her shoulder... rolling her eyes, shaking her head.

Frank said, "You gotta find him, Charlie."

"I know. But I'm afraid he's long gone, Chief." He opened the door and looked outside. "Any word on Hunter King?"

"We're on it, Charlie. You don't have to worry about that right now."

"I know. It's just—"

"It's just *nothing*, Charlie. Don't worry, we're on it."

"It's not about me. It's the people I know he'll go after, he learns I'm the one who shot his brother."

Kim turned to him from the computer. "Charlie? I've got something."

"Listen, Frank. I gotta run."

"Keep me in the loop, Charlie. You hear me?"

"Yeah, I hear you. But there's only so much I can do on the ground. I haven't heard anything in the air outside a couple commercial airlines way up there. If the CMPD air patrol would show up..." He paused, glancing at Kim. "You speak with Monroe PD again? And what about the FBI? I'm surprised... figure with the bomb scare in an airport they would've been here already."

"I can only micromanage so much, Charlie. But if you think I'm just sitting up here twiddling my thumbs..."

Charlie grinned into the phone. "All right, Frank. I'll call you." He hung up the phone and slipped it into his pocket, stepped behind Kim and looked over her shoulder.

She pointed at the computer screen. "This plan here's registered under the name Roger Flynn. It was scheduled to take off twenty minutes ago." She looked out toward the tarmac. "I heard a plane take off. Good chance Jack was on it."

Charlie nodded. "Roger Flynn's a friend of Jack's."

Kim said, "Says here they're headed for Vero Beach, Florida."

Chapter 4

Charlie was behind the wheel, driving Kim's Chevy Tahoe, Kim in the passenger seat next to him staring straight ahead. He looked up in the rearview mirror at Bella, handcuffed in the back seat. "You're looking at a good five years, harboring a fugitive… another five for getting in the way of a federal law enforcement official's duty… maybe ten for assaulting an officer. But if you're willing to talk a little more, tell us where he might've gone…"

Kim turned and looked over her shoulder into the back seat. "Just so you're aware, the trailers will be at your home in the morning. Your horses, your vehicles—including that nice new truck Charlie likes—and whatever else, whether it was there before you got involved with Mr. Thornton or not. It's all going to be gone. And, to me, that's a worse punishment than being behind bars. Because even if your sentence is cut to, say, three-to-five… you'll have nothing left. All because you fell in love with a man who screwed over just about every human he came in contact with."

"He didn't buy everything I own. I worked hard. My family worked hard."

Charlie knew Kim was just trying to put a little more pressure on Bella Ray. He looked in the rearview, saw a tear coming down Bella Ray's cheek. He almost felt bad for her, but he wasn't sure why. He said, "Once they determine what's what—how much of it came from the money Jack stole from all those people and what might've been yours before you got tangled up with him... then maybe it'll be a different story. It'll have to get sorted out in the courts. So right now, your best option is to start talking to us. Or I'm sorry to say you're going to be on your own. There's nothing we'll be able to do to help you."

Bella Ray turned and looked out the back passenger window on her right. After a moment, she turned to Charlie and Kim. "Who's going to protect me?"

Charlie glanced over his shoulder. "You mean if you tell us everything you know?" He paused to think about it, but decided not to answer. "You already mentioned there was more. So, the thing is, the can of worms has pretty much already been opened." He gave her a big smile. "You see what I'm saying?"

Bella Ray held her gaze on him for a moment, turned to her right and looked out the window. "I know there were others involved. He wasn't the only one. I mean, yeah, he was of course right in the middle of it all, but..." She turned back to Charlie. "I'm just telling you there are others."

"Besides his ex-wife and this Roger Flynn fellow?" Charlie said.

"I don't know his ex-wife. He never talked much about her. And I don't think Roger was ever involved, other than putting his name on the plane. He's always seemed like a nice man."

Charlie straightened out in his seat.

Kim turned to him. "Asheville?"

He chewed the inside of his cheek and took a moment before he answered. He looked up in the rearview. "You have someone to take care of your horses? I'm just asking because they'll be arriving early with the trailers."

Bella Ray looked down at her lap, her hands still handcuffed behind her back. "Would it be possible we stop by my house? I do have a farmhand, comes around about this time to feed the horses. But if I could say bye to them..."

Charlie turned to Kim. "You see any problem with that?"

Kim said, "Can we trust her?"

Charlie rubbed the top of his head, still sore from earlier. "Like, will she whack one of us with a spade shovel?" He glanced to his left, watched the farmland and fields go by along 74.

Charlie turned when they got to the mailbox at the end of the dirt driveway. His eyes were already up in the sky on the black clouds of smoke pouring out from somewhere beyond the trees down the long driveway leading to Bella Ray's farmhouse.

"Oh my Lord," Bella Ray said, leaning with her shoulder against the door, her head tilted, eyes up toward the smoke.

Charlie glanced back at her and saw the color had left her face. He said in a hushed voice to Kim, "I've got a bad feeling..."

Another fifty yards and he could see the orange flames, the smoke thicker the farther they drove down the driveway.

Bella Ray cried once they were in view of the barn and the house. "My horses!"

Two horses ran across the tall, uncut grass with another two Charlie spotted in the woods. He saw one lying down, not moving at all. Another ran toward the road as he turned around in the driveway and put the Tahoe in park.

"Oh my God. Please... no!" Bella Ray cried. "Let me out of here. Please!"

Charlie called it in and stepped out from the SUV, walked around the front and opened Bella Ray's door. He held her by the arm as she got her feet down on the ground. "How many you have?" he said.

She stared up at the house, flames coming through the roof. Tears ran down her face. She turned to him with a look of shock and surprise. "Seven. I have seven horses. We have to help them. Please."

The barn was also on fire, a strong odor mixed with the smoke filling the sky. It was more than just wood and hay burning inside. He turned Bella Ray around and removed the handcuffs.

"What are you doing?" Kim said.

He glanced at her, but didn't answer.

Bella Ray ran toward the burning barn.

"Bella Ray!" Charlie yelled, not expecting her to take off like that.

She stopped at one of the horses and wrapped her arms around its neck, crying.

Charlie and Kim ran after her and both jumped and covered their heads when something inside the two-story farmhouse exploded. The roof collapsed. Two horses ran straight into the woods and Charlie counted four still within view, including the one Bella Ray was holding on to. But the explosion startled it and that horse took off for the woods. She took a few steps to run after it, but stopped and cried, calling its name.

Something caught Charlie's eye, at the edge of the woods where one of the remaining horses had stopped. He walked toward it, beyond the burning house and through the smoke sitting over the field. It was almost hard to see until he got far enough from the house and closer to the edge of the woods. He knew, within a few more steps, what had caught his eye. He stopped and waved for Kim to follow him.

He stared down at the body of what looked like a young man on his stomach, face turned to the side with his eyes open. The young man's shirt was soaked in blood. Charlie crouched down next to him and saw the bullet hole, dead center in his back and just below his neck.

Kim walked up behind Charlie as he stood up and turned to her. "Either someone tried to get to Bella Ray... or wanted to send a message."

Bella Ray came running to where they stood over the body. "No!" she cried, dropping to her knees. "Richie! No!" Tears poured down her face. "No!" She turned and looked up at Charlie, stood up and wrapped her arms around his waist, her head buried in his chest.

"Richie?" Charlie said, holding on to Bella Ray with one hand, the other down by his side, by his holster. He glanced at Kim.

Bella Ray sobbed. "Richie took care of my horses. He loved them as much as I did. He was such a good person... who would do this?"

There was another small explosion and the second floor of Bella Ray's house collapsed, the three of them turning to watch. The sirens screamed in the distance, growing louder.

Chapter 5

MOST OF THE PEOPLE on the scene, from the Monroe police to medics and the Union County Sheriff's Office, stood around and watched the firemen point their hoses and soak what was left of Bella Ray's family's farmhouse: not much more than a pile of charred rubble.

The smoke gradually dissipated, the house and the barn both destroyed long before the firemen arrived. Charlie turned when he saw FBI Agent Stan Cooper, the initial lead investigator who brought Jack Thornton down for the Ponzi scheme Jack used to lure hundreds of investors—most of them friends and family—into investing, losing millions of dollars in the process.

Stan shook Charlie's hand and pulled him aside. He kept his voice low, looking around as if to make sure nobody else had been listening. "Tell me I heard the story wrong," he said. "You went from having Thornton four feet in front of you to watching him fly over your head? Then you come back here to see the girlfriend's house and barn on fire... topped off with the farmhand's body with a bullet hole in his back? Did I get that right?"

Charlie took off his hat and fixed his hair. He shifted his stance, folding his arms across his chest. "Funny, because I guess there's something I'm wondering, Stan. And that's how *your* Federal Bureau of Investigations failed to report the girlfriend's life might've been the one in danger?"

Bella Ray stood with Kim in the field between the house and the barn—what was left of them—tears in her eyes, holding on to a long rope tied to the only horse that hadn't run off into the woods.

Stan nodded toward Bella Ray and turned back to Charlie. "You going to be keeping an eye on her for me?" He cracked a slight smile. "Consider yourself lucky. You're not married anymore, is that right?"

Charlie held his gaze on Stan for a moment, knew Stan was just trying to say something to sound cool, maybe pull back on some of the hostility he sent Charlie's way. But Stan's sense of humor was lacking. Somewhat of a nerd, as far as Charlie was concerned; wouldn't know what to do with a woman like Bella Ray if he had an instruction manual.

"So what're you thinking?" Charlie said. "Someone came here looking for Jack? Or you think this is his doing, send someone in and make sure Bella Ray keeps her mouth shut?"

Stan took a moment before he answered. "We investigated Jack Thornton for eighteen months. He was a loner who didn't trust many people. I mean, he had people working for him—a friend or two he could trust, but"—Stan shook his head—"Jack's the one we want. We were never able to find evidence to suggest Bella Ray was anything other than a young lady trying to latch on to a man like Jack, enough money she wouldn't have to worry about a thing besides playing with her horses all day."

"You think she's lying?" Charlie said.

Stan took a moment, looking back over at Bella Ray. "She's worried about keeping that ass of hers out of jail. Nothing more to it, you ask me."

Charlie said, "You say nobody else was involved. But what do you know about Elizabeth Thornton?"

"The ex?" Stan shook his head. "She might've flown him out of the airport—and she'll certainly pay for her involvement—but we brought her in at one point, had her under surveillance for six months. I'm not sure she and Jack even spoke. Not until recently. I was surprised to hear she was at that airport."

Charlie rubbed the stubble on his face. "But she could've been involved the whole time?" he said. "Just because you don't have any evidence doesn't mean—"

"I just told you she was on our radar," Stan said. "But if she indeed was the one flying that plane, then it'll be the first and only time we can put her together with Jack over the past eighteen months."

Charlie looked up the hill, his eyes on the coroner's van. "And what about Roger Flynn?"

Stan nodded. "Clean, as far as we know."

"As far as you know? Man has his name on a plane belongs to a fugitive."

"We believe Jack put Roger Flynn's name on it, just to keep it off our radar."

"Okay, so then would you admit you have no idea if this is Jack's doing or someone who might've been after him?"

Stan nodded. "Charlie, if I had an easy button I could push and the answer would pop out, you'd be free to use it. But, no, we don't know if Jack did this to keep Bella Ray from talking, or someone maybe sending a message to Jack."

"But if nobody else was involved with Jack..." Charlie stopped himself, knowing Stan would be ready to shut him off.

Stan said, "Jack had only been back here for a few days. Maybe the same person who shared his location with us shared it with someone else. We don't have that answer yet. But I'll be sure to let you know when we have it." He turned and started to walk away, then stopped and looked back at Charlie. "If you wanted to ask all these questions, why didn't you work with us, instead of becoming a U.S. Marshal?"

It was dark when Kim and Charlie drove away—Kim behind the wheel this time, Bella Ray in the back seat again with her eyes on the four horses they'd found in the woods, roped to a truck parked in the field.

Bella Ray cried. "Why won't you let me go look for the other horses?" She turned, straightened herself out in the seat but kept her gaze out the passenger-side window behind Charlie.

Without looking back, Charlie said, "Because we have men and women looking for them. Men and women we don't have to worry'll try to run off."

He glanced at Kim behind the wheel and focused on the ride ahead of them.

It was late, almost dark, and the day had grown longer and later than either of them had expected it would.

"How long are you going to hold me?" Bella Ray said. "I want to be able to look through the house—what's left of it—see what can be saved."

Kim glanced at Charlie, gave him a look he'd seen before. She'd let him answer the questions.

"I don't think you understand all that's happened so far," Charlie said. He turned to Bella Ray. "You're going to need to do a lot more talking when we get back to Asheville so we can find your boyfriend. But you need to keep in mind you've done some things you probably shouldn't have done. I don't know much about your past, but I'll just assume it took a turn in the wrong direction the day you met Jack Thornton."

Kim looked in the rearview, her eyes on Bella Ray. "You should realize how lucky you are you weren't in that house. Or that you weren't the one to get a bullet in the back, like your friend." She shifted her eyes to the road. "And I assure you, if you weren't such a pretty young woman, Deputy Harlow here wouldn't have been so easy on you, helping your boyfriend escape. I've seen how he can react to people doing lesser things to him than that."

"I said I was sorry. I just—"

"What we're saying, Bella Ray, is some of what'll happen to you may be out of our hands. But we'll do what we can to help you if you're willing to cooperate."

Bella Ray said, "I promised you already. I will. Whatever I can do to help. You think I'm going to try protect whoever it was did that to my home? To my horses?"

"You'll help us find Jack?" Charlie said, turning in his seat to look Bella Ray in the eye.

She stared back at him and nodded, but didn't say another word for the rest of the ride back to Asheville.

Chapter 6

Deputy Chief Frank Carter was already seated in the small conference room, leaning with his elbows on the glass table, papers in his hands, when Charlie and Kim walked in with Bella Ray. He removed his reading glasses and leaned back in the chair, folded his arms across his chest. He watched the three sit on the other side of the table, looked from Kim to Charlie. "Why is it you two always have a way of turning every molehill you come across into a mountain?"

Charlie chose to ignore Frank's comment. "Frank," he said, "as I'm sure you're aware, this here is Miss Bella Ray Sparrow. Jack Thornton's girlfriend."

Frank stared at her. "Is that how you'd like to be addressed? The girlfriend of Jack Thornton, a wanted man?" He put his reading glasses back on his face and opened the folder in front of him. He moved his finger down the first sheet of paper on top, looked up at Charlie over his glasses. "How come I don't see any mention of a shovel?"

Charlie leaned with both arms down on the table. "Well, I'd promised Miss Sparrow we'd be able to discuss how much I enter into the system about what happened, dependent on what she decides to tell us today."

Frank turned his eyes back to Bella. "You do realize there's quite a penalty involved when you strike a law enforcement officer? Especially when he's engaged in the performance of his official duty and you obstruct the apprehension of a known fugitive?"

Bella Ray had her eyes down on her hands clasped together on the table. She looked up at Frank and nodded. "Yes, sir. I am truly sorry for what I—"

"*Sorry* does not matter right now, my dear," Frank said. He leaned back in his chair and pushed himself back from the table. "You'd be looking at up to ten years, ma'am. In a federal prison, max security. But I do understand Deputy Harlow believes you know where your boyfriend might've gone. And if you're willing to lead us to him..." He leaned forward and closed the folder. "I can see what we can do about making sure your actions are kept between everyone right here at this table."

Bella Ray looked at Charlie and Kim, her hands still clasped together, her fingertips red she had squeezed them so tight. "Are you going to find whoever it was burned down my home and killed Richie?"

"Richie?" Frank said. "He your farmhand?"

"He was a good man," she said. "He didn't deserve this."

Charlie thought that was quite the understatement. "Bella Ray, you need to give us any and all names you can think of who may've been involved all along. Or anyone who, perhaps, might've been looking for the money Jack obtained illegally."

Frank cleared his throat. "Deputy Harlow likes to play detective, but it's not the duty of the U.S. Marshals Service to investigate or solve crimes. Apprehending federal fugitives like Mr. Thornton falls in the lap of the USMS." He smiled, almost a smirk. "It's our specialty. We bring in the bad guys, then move on to the next case."

Bella Ray turned to Charlie. "You said it might've been someone sending a message. You must have…"

"I did say that," Charlie said. "But I'm only making assumptions right now. The FBI is involved, cooperating in the investigation with the Monroe Police and the Union County Sheriff's Office."

"Your boyfriend wasn't a good man," Kim said. "Men who do bad things to other people usually hang around with other bad people. So we need you to think good and hard about who those people might be."

"It'll also be our job to protect you," Charlie said. "But you need to help us so we can help you. And you need to realize Jack Thornton's got his own interests in mind at this point. It's very likely he's the one who did that to your home. And those beautiful horses."

Bella Ray shook her head. "Jack wouldn't do that. He couldn't have."

Charlie said, "Just because he was on a plane heading for who knows where doesn't mean he didn't make the call."

"He also could've been trying to hide or destroy evidence he may have left behind," Frank said. He leaned forward, looked across at Bella Ray. "People have all sorts of reasons for burning things down. And maybe, just spit-balling here, maybe your friend, the farmhand, just happened to've been in the wrong place at the wrong time. Chances are he witnessed whoever it was lit those fires—one of Jack's associates or not—and someone made sure he wouldn't be around to talk about what he saw."

A tear came down Bella Ray's face. She leaned back in her chair and folded her arms, squeezing them tight against her body, just under her chest.

Charlie glanced at Frank and gave a quick nod to Kim. He knew the pressure the three of them were putting on Bella Ray seemed to be working... turn her against the boyfriend, and things would only get easier.

But he could see Bella's wheels were still turning. "I don't understand why Jack would... I mean, he was home all morning before you showed up. Don't you think if he was planning to do something like this, he would have—"

"Jack had a bag packed in the trunk of his car," Kim said. "He had planned to leave. But by the sounds of it, you may not've been part of those plans. That plane, and his ex-wife, were waiting for him. All we might've done was push up the schedule by a few minutes."

Bella Ray just stared back at Kim, her mouth open like she had something to say, but nothing came out.

Frank got up from the table. "Can I speak to the two of you in my office?" He walked out the door.

Charlie turned to Bella before he and Kim stepped out into the hall. "Give us a moment. And don't try and leave... you won't get very far." He closed the door and walked behind Kim into Frank's office.

Frank said, "This girl might not know a thing. And we need to be careful before we make too many promises to her we all know we won't be able to keep. She struck a U.S. Marshal with a shovel. No judge is gonna let that slide, Charlie."

Charlie grinned. "Don't worry, Frank. It's all there in the report."

Frank smiled. "I know it is. I'm just doing my best to let her believe you're the one on her side."

Kim said, "We have anyone looking down Vero Beach?"

Frank nodded. "Nobody showed up at the airport down there."

Charlie said, "Plane that size could've landed anywhere... in a field, or..." He thought for a moment. "What if we take Bella Ray down to Florida, see if somehow she can draw him out for us?"

"Are you serious?" Frank said.

Charlie shrugged. "She must know something, maybe where he'd be. Get her down there, make him believe we let her go…"

"Too dangerous," Kim said.

The three stood quiet for a couple of moments.

Charlie looked at his watch and said to Frank, "You talk to anyone at the Bureau?"

Frank paused, shook his head. "Why don't you get Stan on the horn, see if they have any clues as to what might've happened at that house?"

All three turned when Bella Ray knocked on the edge of the door's molding from the hallway outside. "I'm sorry, but I've got to use the ladies' room, if that's all right?"

Frank looked at Kim. "Mind taking her down the hall?"

Kim stepped out from the office. "Follow me."

Charlie waited a moment until Kim and Bella Ray were out of sight. "She seems too sweet to be tied up with a man like Jack Thornton, don't you think?"

"She's a southern girl," Frank said. "Can turn it on when she needs to. I'd like to think you'd have your radar on, not let a pretty girl fool you like that."

Charlie rolled his eyes and turned to the door, poked his head out and looked down the hall toward the restrooms. He turned back to Frank. "Nah, when I say *sweet*, I'm not saying I can't see through it. And I'm starting to think she's a lot smarter than she'd like any of us—including Jack Thornton himself—to believe."

"What are you saying?" Frank said.

Charlie rubbed the back of his head, still sore from the shovel. "Someone's gotta keep a real good eye on her. Either that or we lock her up."

Frank had a look on his face, curious about where Charlie was heading. "I don't see why she shouldn't spend the night behind bars," he said. "It's not worth the risk."

Charlie shook his head. "All we'll have to go through to get her out of there in the morning... Thornton'll be two days ahead of us."

"So what do you suggest?" Frank said. "You going to take her home with you?"

"Come on, Frank. I'm just saying, we put her in the Hampton Inn, put a man or two on the door until morning."

"We don't have an extra man," Frank said. "Oh, I might have one. Maybe Gilson."

Gilson?" Charlie said, shaking his head. "He all you have?"

Frank shrugged and nodded. "Either that or she spends the night in the cell."

Chapter 7

Charlie glanced at the mailbox with HARLOW painted on the side and turned into the driveway of the small, white ranch. He stepped out and admired the large, flowered shrubs and the rose bushes he remembered planting along the front of the house. Colorful flowers ran along both sides of the walkway leading up to the front door, where a hanging plant with purple buds hung on a hook opposite the American flag.

He reached into his pocket for his keys, but the interior door opened.

Jennie looked good, as always, standing there behind the screen watching Charlie. She held open the storm door.

"Thanks for waiting for me," Charlie said, stepping inside. He followed her into the kitchen. "You look nice." His nose caught the same sweet perfume she'd always worn, back before they were first married. He liked it. And missed it. But knew one compliment for the early morning was enough.

She grabbed her cup of coffee and took a sip, leaned back against the front of the sink and stared back at him over the rim. "You want a drink?"

Charlie shook his head. "No, I'm good."

She turned and looked out the window behind the sink into the backyard, up on her toes to get a better look when something must have caught her eye. "So what is it, Charlie?" She turned to him and placed her cup on the counter next to the sink.

Charlie took off his hat and fixed the front of his hair, pushing it off his forehead. "We're going to have a couple of deputy marshals down here to keep an eye on the house for a little while."

Jennie closed her eyes and moved a strand of hair from her face. "Jesus, Charlie. Keep an eye on the house? Or on *me*?"

Charlie shifted his stance and took a moment before he answered. "You know that man who shot the deputy in Candler when we were delivering the warrant?"

Jennie nodded. "You shot him, didn't you? Not the deputy, but—"

"Yeah, well, there's a second suspect, although we still haven't located him. In fact, now we don't know if the man I shot's the one who pulled the trigger or not."

Jennie's started to say something but stayed quiet, her mouth still open a bit.

Charlie looked down at his hat, still in his hand, and raised his eyes back to Jennie. "We believe the second suspect's the brother. And until we find him..."

Jennie put her hands on her hips. "Are you telling me I need to sleep with one eye open... as if I don't do that already?"

Charlie shrugged. "Like I said, we're going to have someone here for a few days, keep an eye on things. I'd like to tell you it'd be me, but I'm going to be heading out of town."

She shook her head. "Jesus, Charlie. We're not even together anymore, but I'm still living in the nightmare I'd hoped to escape. It's like I'm trapped in this crazy life because you—"

"I will always be there to protect you, Jennie. And, the truth is, it's just a precaution. Frank agreed it was a good idea, at least until we can locate Hunter King."

"Hunter? That's his name?"

Charlie nodded. "Brother I shot's name was Gunner. Clearly, they were raised having a thing for guns." He smiled, but Jennie didn't appear to find it funny.

"And now you're going out of town? How does that fall under 'I'll always be there to protect you'? You leave and someone else has to clean up your mess." She shook her head and turned to the window over the sink. "You have a very short list of people you've loved. Sometimes I think I'd be better off if I wasn't on it."

"You use the word 'love'—past tense. But you know I still love you. I'm not the one who wanted a divorce."

She turned to him and ran her tongue inside her cheek. "You're not the one who wanted it. But you're certainly the one who caused it."

Charlie took a deep breath and exhaled with a sigh, turning toward the door. "I just want you to know you'll be safe," he said. "I know how much you enjoy your privacy, but…" He took a step away from her. "Hopefully it'll be a short-term thing." He got to the door and pulled it open.

"Where are you going?" Jennie said.

"Back to Asheville."

"I mean, you said you'd be gone for a few days. Where're you going to be?"

Oh, uh… Florida."

She raised her voice a bit more. "You're going to Florida? And you're telling me I have to—"

"Business," he said. "Fugitive slipped through my fingers yesterday and now it's up to me to find him." He leaned down and pointed to the wound on his head. "His girlfriend whacked me on the head with a shovel."

She nodded, not showing much concern for his injury. "Crossed my mind to do that a few times." She appeared to try to hold back her smile, but couldn't stop it.

"I'll only be gone a few days."

She laughed. "How many times have I heard that one? Come back a month later..."

Charlie stared back at her, liked the way she played. He liked her blue eyes, her tan skin, the way she wore her makeup—not too much—and always had her hair up on her head unless she was getting dressed up. "You be careful, okay?"

She nodded. "*You* be careful, Charlie."

He pulled on the door and stopped one more time. "You have Frank's direct line, don't you? And his cell, if you need anything?"

Jennie turned and picked up her cup of coffee. "I'll be fine. Bye, Charlie."

Charlie jumped on 26 heading back to the office and called Frank from the car.

"How'd she take it?" Frank said, his first words as he answered.

"She wasn't happy about it, of course. I didn't expect much else."

"Don't worry about her. We won't let her out of our sight."

"Yeah, that's the part she's not happy about." Charlie reached for the can of soda he had in the cupholder in the center console, took a sip but struggled to get it down it was so warm and flat. "Any word on Hunter King?"

"Nothing," Frank said. "He's around; whether he shows his face or not, we'll find him. Asheville PD, Buncombe County Sheriff's Office... we're all working together to shake the trees. We'll get him. Don't you worry."

"I'm not so much worried. I just don't like being on the outside when something involves me like this. I should be out there looking for him before he gets to me. Or Jennie. I don't see why we can't just let them down there in the Southern District of Florida to go after Thornton."

Frank said, "I told you, they're short-manned. And you should feel lucky you still have your badge while the bureau investigates. Secondly, you're already booked for Florida. Just do me a favor. Get this son-of-a-bitch Thornton, so I can get this off my desk. Do whatever you have to... Wait, I didn't mean that. Please don't take what I just said literally, Charlie."

Charlie smiled, relaxed, his wrist resting on the top of the steering wheel. "I'll see you at the office before I go."

Frank said, "Aren't you going by the hotel to pick up Bella Ray?"

"Kim was going to get her, meet me at the office at ten."

"It's nine forty-five," Frank said.

"Then she should be there in fifteen minutes."

Frank said, "You haven't talked to her?" He sounded concerned. "Do me a favor and give her a call; make sure everything's all right over there."

"I can do that," Charlie said just as another call came in on the other line. "Hang on a second, Frank." He glanced at the screen. "There's Kim calling right now. I'm sure everything's fine." He paused a moment. "I'll call you back." He ended the call with Frank and answered the other line. "Kim?"

"Where are you?" she said.

Charlie could sense something wrong in her voice. "I'm on Twenty-Six. Everything all right?"

"No, it's not, Charlie. She's not here."

"Who's not where?"

"Bella Ray. I came to pick her up at the Hampton Inn. She's gone.

Chapter 8

CHARLIE STEPPED FROM HIS car and walked toward Frank, already in the parking lot standing next to Kim and two officers outside the Hampton Inn. "What the hell happened?" Charlie said, walking past the two locals as they turned away from Frank.

Kim waited until Charlie got closer to answer. "I was actually early," she said. "Got here fifteen minutes before I said I would, at nine thirty. Gilson's standing outside the door, business as usual. I knock, Bella Ray doesn't answer."

Charlie looked up along the side of the hotel. "What floor?"

"Room six oh four. Gave it another minute before I knocked again, thinking maybe she'd been in the shower. But finally slipped the passkey in the lock... bed's made like she'd never even gone to sleep. No sign at all she'd been in the room."

Charlie eyed Frank scratching the top of his head. "What'd he say? How the hell'd he—"

"Gilson?" Kim shrugged. "Said he never left his post at the door."

Charlie again looked up the building at the sixth-floor windows. "He still drink coffee by the pot?" He looked at Frank. "You know what I'm asking, don't you, Frank?"

Frank and Kim exchanged a look, but neither answered.

"What I'm saying is I'd be willing to guess Gilson snuck off to take a piss. Bella Ray had her eye on the peephole all night, waiting for her chance, hoping he'd walk away."

Frank said, "I gotta believe Gilson, says he didn't leave his post."

"Do you?" Charlie said, giving the chief a look.

"Small window of time, but it's also possible she was abducted." Frank said.

Charlie rubbed the back of his neck, feeling tight from all the driving and looking up the building. "Makes even less sense, someone waiting all night for the chance to take her out of there. Although the one thing I'd say I'm sure of is Gilson left and took a leak. So either way..." He took a step toward the hotel and turned back to Frank and Kim. "I fell for her act... now I'd have to say she had this planned the whole time."

"And now you know why I said we shoulda locked her up," Frank said.

Charlie nodded, knowing it was on him. He knew better.

Frank said, "Now don't go in there taking it out on Gilson. I'll talk to him later. He's not feeling too good about things right now."

"Good," Charlie said. "He shouldn't feel good about *anything*."

"I'm not sure it's entirely his fault," Kim said. "He supposed to hold it all night?"

Charlie nodded. "Yes." He stepped to the sliding doors of the hotel and walked through, but stopped in the lobby and walked back out to Frank and Kim. "You know, maybe we should get someone down there to check on her house. Wouldn't put it past her she—"

"For what?" Frank said. "There's nothing left. Horses are all rounded up, going out to auction this weekend. House was burnt to the ground, only thing standing is the concrete around the basement. Investigators are still there now, trying to determine what exactly happened. She'd be foolish to go there."

"What about the airport?" Charlie said. "We got anyone over there? Monroe PD? Or Union County Sheriff's Office?"

Kim said, "I don't think she'd be that foolish."

"It's not like she's getting a commercial flight out of here," Charlie said. "I think she's the type do something we wouldn't expect 'cause it'd be something only a fool would do. Just something I think we should be sure of. You never know…"

Frank said, "I'm still not ready to rule out an abduction. Asheville PD's investigating, going through camera footage, talking to employees who were here through the night."

Charlie looked toward the hotel through the glass doors and into the lobby. He was going to go in himself and start asking questions but didn't want to step on anyone's toes at the Asheville PD. Frank hated when he played investigator, anyway. "So this change any of our plans?" he said.

Frank shook his head. "Not in the least. They're expecting you, got a space set up in the Florida office. But like I said, they're shorthanded." He nodded at Kim. "It'll just be the two of you."

Kim and Charlie took the elevator to their office on the third floor of the courthouse and stepped off where two deputy marshals were waiting in the hall.

"Lost another one, eh, Charlie," one of them said, a smirk on his face.

Charlie wanted to knock the son of a bitch's head off, stood chest to chest with him.

Kim pulled him back by the arm. "Come on," she said. "We've got work to do." She didn't let go until they were in front of their office. "You know he does it to everyone."

Charlie nodded and glanced back over his shoulder, but the elevator doors had already closed with the two deputy marshals inside. "Yeah, and nobody says a goddamn word to him. One of these days someone's gonna have to knock that shit-eatin' grin off his face. Can't see why it shouldn't be me." He turned the knob and pushed open the glass door, stopped and let Kim walk in ahead of him.

She stepped past the cubicles and turned toward her desk. "Just remember why he has this job in the first place. And he wouldn't know what to do if he ever had to step outside that courtroom."

Charlie smiled, about to sit down at his desk when his phone rang. "It's Frank." He answered. "Hey, Chief."

"Charlie, just got off the phone with South District down in Florida. Had a couple of deputy marshals spend a few hours tracking flights, said there's no chance Jack Thornton's plane ever touched down in Vero Beach."

Charlie closed his eyes, shaking his head. "You gotta be shitting me."

"I wish I was."

"So where is it?"

"Well, you happen to see that plane was registered in Aruba?"

"Meaning there's no tracking?" Charlie said.

"You got it."

Kim stood next to Charlie's desk.

Charlie said, "Then how can they be so sure he didn't fly in under the radar?"

"I don't have that answer. They sounded sure of themselves," Frank said. "I don't know what else to tell you. Other than we've gotta find a way to track this plane down."

Charlie nodded into the phone, ran his hand over his tired eyes. "No tracking? No tail number? How are we supposed to—"

Frank said, "You ever think it's possible Jack never got on that plane in the first place?"

Charlie glanced at Kim and said into the phone, "But Kim saw him get..." He pulled the phone away from his ear, pressed it against his chest. "Frank's asking if there's a chance Jack Thornton never got on that plane. You saw him get on it, isn't that right?"

Kim swallowed and stared back at Charlie without saying a word.

He could see it in her eyes she was questioning herself whether she had seen it or not. He put the phone up to his face. "She was tied up in the hangar, Frank. She might've seen him get on but that doesn't mean he didn't get off. But you bring up a... the slippery son of a bitch could be right here in North Carolina."

Kim said to Charlie, "Maybe he waited for Bella Ray, in a car now headed south."

Charlie gazed back at her, nodding as he listened to Frank on the other end.

"I'm on my way back to the office now," Frank said. "Sit tight until I get there, before this gets any more out of control."

Chapter 9

Kim had collected the files on Jack Thornton's ex-wife, Elizabeth, and dropped them in a folder down on the table between Frank and Charlie. She pulled up a chair and sat next to Frank. "Elizabeth Thornton, friends call her 'Liz.' She owns a small home on Amelia Island, down Northeast Florida. Fernandina Beach PD checked it out... turns out she doesn't live there. Rents to an older couple who don't seem to know much about her."

Charlie leaned back in his chair, his hands clasped together holding the back of his head. "They ask where they mail their rent?"

Kim nodded. "Money gets wired from their account to an international account... bank based out of San Marino."

"Italy?" Frank said, shaking his head. "Slippery as her ex-husband."

"What about the friend?" Charlie said, straightening out in the chair, reaching for the folder.

Kim nodded toward the folder in Charlie's hands. "Roger Flynn's sixty-seven years old, has a house in Miami and another up in Maine. Kennebunkport. Couple of kids, both grown and don't seem to talk to him anymore. Nobody's seen him at either of his two houses in the past three weeks."

Frank counted on his hand, "Jack Thornton, Elizabeth Thornton, Roger Flynn, and our girl... Bella Ray Sparrow. We've got our hands full now."

"But we don't know if they're all together at this point, either," Kim said. "Roger Flynn may've only been out in Aruba to register Jack's plane."

"Could still be there," Charlie said, glancing at Frank running his hands over his face. "You all right, Frank?"

He nodded. "I'm getting too old for this shit."

"Maybe we oughta go to Aruba," Charlie said, a big smile on his face.

Frank nodded, like he liked the idea. "I don't know if I'd ever come back." He stood up from his chair and turned from the table. "You two do me a favor, see what kind of connection you can draw to any of these four. Relatives, old friends, ex-lovers... anything we can come up with where Jack—or all four—may be hiding." He pulled open the door and left the office.

Charlie leaned on the table and gave Kim a nod. "How sure are we this Roger Flynn's not around either of his homes? Are they both empty? Or—"

"Miami police confirmed, as did Kennebunkport PD. Both are keeping an eye out, in case anyone shows up."

"And where do these grown kids of his live?"

"Has a daughter—thirty-two-years-old—lives in Paris. Son is twenty-nine, last known address just happens to be over in Charlotte. Worked for the Bank of America."

"Worked? Past tense?"

"I don't have that answer," Kim said. "Waiting on it."

Charlie looked down at the folder, flipped through the pages inside. "Roger Flynn's in some kind of financial service business, is that right?"

Kim grinned. "Of course he is. They're all in some kind of financial service... banking. They get the taste of the green. Money's like heroine to these kind of people. They know they don't need any more to live a normal life, but can't help themselves."

"But financial services is a pretty broad industry. I imagine he wasn't workin' as a teller at a local bank, buying two homes on the water."

Kim grabbed the folder from in front of Charlie and flipped through the sheets of paper inside. She pulled one from the stack, held it up in front of her. "Banking Consultant," she said. "Company was dissolved last year. Called Flynn and Company." She looked over the page at Charlie. "Didn't you read any of this?"

He gave her a blank look and nodded. "Yeah, of course." He shrugged. "Some of it."

"Then you know Jack Thornton was VP of Flynn's company, don't you?"

"VP? Recently?"

Kim shook her head. "Five years ago."

Charlie removed his hat and scratched his head. "I'm sorry. I spent time on the road, went down made sure Jennie knew she'd have some company for a little while."

"How'd she take it?" Kim said.

"As good as you'd expect her to."

"Not good, huh?"

Charlie smiled and shook his head.

Kim got up from the chair and walked to the window overlooking the parking lot. "I'm sorry," she said. "I should've been more careful when Jack snuck up on me like he did. I wish I'd—"

"I second-guessed every move I made, I'd never stop beating myself up. But we just don't get the kind of time we need to wallow in our sorrows." He stood up and rolled his chair in under the table. "Speaking of second-guessing"—he looked through the glass toward the rest of the office—"if this wild-goose chase's going to be on hold for now, I might see if Frank'll let me spend some time helping track down Hunter King."

Kim gave Charlie a serious look. "No chance, Charlie. I wouldn't even ask. You know it's out of Frank's hands anyway."

"We don't find him soon, he's going to show up when I'm not expecting him. Or he'll use Jennie to draw me to him." He pulled open the door and stepped out from the conference room, straight out the office and down the hall.

Kim followed and stood next to him in front of the elevator. "I don't understand why he's been so hard to find," she said.

Charlie had his eyes up on the illuminated arrow above the doors. "Who, Hunter?" he glanced at her until the elevator bell rang.

Kyle Rivers—nephew of Congressman Chet Rivers—stepped through the doors into the hall. He smiled at Charlie—more of a smirk—and looked Kim up and down. He kept walking without saying a word to either of them.

Charlie and Kim both glanced at each other and stepped into the elevator.

Kim said, "You don't smack him one of these days, I just might have to do it myself next time he looks at me like that."

The doors started to close and Frank yelled for them to hold it.

Charlie stuck his foot out and stopped the door before it closed, using his hand to push it open. "Chief?" he said.

Frank stood outside in the hall, breathing heavy and leaning with his hand against the wall just outside the doors. He seemed to almost choke for air as he spoke.

"Bella... Bella Ray Sparrow was possibly spotted getting off a bus in Greenville."

"How long ago?" Charlie said, stepping off the elevator and Kim right behind him.

Frank seemed to want to get his breathing slowed down, took a moment to answer. "Ten thirty this morning. Got off the bus and into a taxi. Couple of Greenville officers realized she was the same woman from the APB, but she was already gone."

Kim said, "Miss Union County'd better dirty herself up a little more, she doesn't want people to recognize a pretty face like that."

Frank and Charlie both glanced at Kim at the same time and headed back to the office.

Charlie said, "So are we heading down to Greenville?"

Frank pushed open the office door and looked back at Charlie over his shoulder. "One of you call the cab company, see if they can be of any help... maybe get the location they dropped her off."

Kim said, "She could be long gone by now. Who knows if she got on a plane out there, or—"

"If it's the bus station I'm thinking of, right there in Greenville, you're talking a twenty-minute drive to GSP Airport."

Frank nodded at Kim. "Check the morning and early-afternoon flights; see what options we have."

Kim pulled out her phone, tapped the screen a few times and placed the phone on the table between her and Charlie. She looked down. "Departures out of GSP." She tapped the screen. "Atlanta at ten thirty. Too early; she wouldn't have made it." She tapped the screen again. "Eleven o'clock flight to Charlotte." She looked up at Charlie, shaking her head. "Makes no sense for her to fly to Charlotte." She tapped the screen again. "Here's one... eleven-twenty to Fort Lauderdale."

Charlie glanced over at Frank standing over the photocopy machine. "Frank, looks like there's an eleven-twenty flight to Fort Lauderdale."

Frank looked at his watch. "Could be it. But she'd be long gone by now, even if we could get someone over there." He scratched his head. "Could've gone down to Miami..."

"Or up to Palm Beach," Kim said.

"Maybe Kim's right," Frank said. "Go to Greenville, talk to the cabbie. Head over to GSP and fly to Fort Lauderdale from there."

"You don't think we need a little more than this?" Charlie said. "She could be anywhere."

Frank shook his head. "We confirm she was on that flight, we'll have a pretty good idea at least what region she's gone to. Besides, we wait around much longer, Jack Thornton'll be out of the country. If he's not already."

"Well," Charlie said, "Let's just hope he decides to wait for Miss Union County before he disappears."

Chapter 10

Charlie drove his Crown Victoria down to Greenville with Kim, parked in front of the brick building with the three yellow garage doors, the *Yellow Cab* sign on a yellow awning over a door with *Entrance* spelled out with stickers.

Charlie's phone rang as he reached for the door. He answered, "Charlie Harlow."

"Charlie, it's Stan Cooper. I don't know what you've heard so far, but the locals down there in Monroe have confirmed the fire at the Sparrow residence to be arson."

"Should I be surprised?" Charlie said.

"Of course not. But a neighbor down the road from the house claimed to've seen a dark Mercedes leaving the property before she'd noticed the fire. She didn't recognize the car, said not many people drive down the private road."

"That mean anything to you?" Charlie said, giving Kim a look, the phone up to his ear.

"Man fits the description of Roger Flynn was seen filling five-gallon containers of gasoline at a station over in Waxhaw—next town over—and was coincidentally driving a black Mercedes."

"Who'd you talk to? Monroe PD?" Charlie said.

"Union County Sheriff's Office. Deputy out there noticed the man, I guess found it odd… Wouldn't look twice had he seen a country boy in work boots and a tank top filling five-gallon containers, loading them into a pickup. But a man looks like he's got some money, sticking containers in the trunk of his Mercedes… the deputy took notice."

"I appreciate the call."

"Any luck locating Miss Sparrow?"

"We're thinking she may've gotten on a flight out of here, but still waiting for confirmation. We're in Greenville right now, about to go talk to the cabbie who might've given her a ride from the bus station. I'll let you know we get anywhere, if you'd like?"

"If you would, I'd appreciate it. But I'll be happy when we get our hands on Jack Thornton."

Charlie hung up, stuck the phone in his pants pocket and walked to the door with Kim. "That was Stan. Monroe PD confirmed the fire was arson."

"Not a surprise," Kim said.

"Yeah, but take a guess who was spotted at a gas station in Waxhaw?"

Kim stared back at him. "Are you going to tell me?"

"Roger Flynn. Allegedly," Charlie said.

"Roger Flynn? So he's not in Aruba?"

"If it was him, then he shot the farmhand. Maybe the kid surprised him, Roger did what he had to make sure he didn't talk."

"But this is all speculation," Kim said.

Charlie nodded and pulled open the glass door, let Kim walk in ahead of him.

They both stood together at the service counter, an older gentleman seated on a stool at the other side, reading a magazine.

Charlie pulled out his badge. "Sir?"

The old man looked up like he didn't even know they were there. "Yes?"

"I'm Deputy U.S. Marshal Charlie Harlow. This is Deputy Marshal Kim Riggins. I called earlier, spoke to someone about a passenger was picked up by one of your cabs from the bus station downtown?"

The man shrugged. "I don't know. If you're telling me you called, then I believe you. But you didn't talk to me."

Charlie looked around, not much to look at other than a wall behind them and a door at the other end of it. The walls were painted yellow, nothing on them but a clock up over the door. It smelled like one of those pine tree air fresheners and car exhaust. "You sure I didn't talk to you?" he said, thinking the man's voice sounded like the one he'd heard.

The man put up a finger and walked around from the other side of the counter, continued toward the door at the back and opened it. He stuck his head through the opening and said something Charlie couldn't hear.

A woman of Indian decent came through the door behind the man and smiled at Charlie. "Can I help you?"

Charlie nodded. "I spoke with a gentleman here about an hour ago, wanting to talk to the driver who might've given a young woman a ride from the bus station."

The woman smiled. "Ah, yes. That was AJ you spoke to. But I'm sorry, he's not here right now." She looked up at the clock over the door. "He'll be back in an hour."

Charlie looked at his watch, even though he knew what time it was with the clock right there in front of him.

Kim said to the woman, "Was AJ the driver?"

The woman walked around the other side of the service counter where the man was back on the stool reading the magazine, paying no attention to anyone else. She leaned over the computer and moved the mouse around, clicked a button on the keyboard and turned back to Charlie and Kim. She shook her head. "No, I believe the driver was Veejay."

"Any chance Veejay's around for us to talk to him?"

Charlie and Kim gave each other a quick glance, Charlie feeling like it should be easier to get what they were looking for.

But the woman nodded. "I believe he's out back. One of the cars drove in before I came out here, and I'd guess it's Veejay."

"It's an urgent matter," Kim said, "if you don't mind pointing us his way?"

She looked from Charlie to Kim. The smile left her face. "Are you the police?" she said.

"No ma'am. We're with the U.S. Marshals Service."

She held her gaze for a moment then nodded and turned from them, walking back through the door she'd just walked out from.

Charlie's phone rang. He looked at the screen. "It's Frank." He answered, "Chief, what've you got?"

"Nothing. No record of Bella Ray being on any flights out of that airport. Doesn't mean she didn't fly out of there. Never know... could've slipped on a plane somehow or, who knows, hopped on a private jet."

"One waiting for her," Charlie said. "Roger Flynn."

The woman walked through the door again with an older Indian gentleman behind her.

"Frank, let me call you back." He hung up and nodded toward the man. "You must be Veejay?"

The man smiled and nodded but didn't speak a word.

Charlie showed his badge once again, introduced himself and Kim and pulled out the photo of Bella Ray Sparrow. "You recognize this woman? She may've gotten in your cab from the bus station?"

The man took the picture, studied it for a moment, then handed it back to Charlie. He nodded. "Yes."

"Did you drive her to the airport?"

Veejay glanced at the woman standing next to him, then back to Charlie. "Yes."

"She tell you anything? Where she might've been going? Anything at all?" Charlie had his voice raised, as if that made a difference if there were a possible language barrier. He wasn't sure there was.

The man shook his head. "I dropped her off at arrivals, at the lower level."

Charlie looked at Kim.

Kim said to the man, "She mention anything about where she was going? Maybe vacation, or—"

"I'm not even sure she went inside. She didn't have any luggage or anything. Strange. I drove away and watched in my mirror. She walked right by the sliding doors, walked along the terminal."

"So she didn't go inside?"

The man shrugged. "I don't think so."

"You see any cars? You notice her talk to anyone?"

Veejay looked to be thinking. "Like I said, it was arrivals. There were service vehicles. Cabs. Other than that, I—"

"You happen to notice a black Mercedes?"

He paused, as if thinking. He nodded. "Yes."

"You sure?" Charlie said.

"Yes."

Charlie reached out and shook the man's hand, then shook the woman's. "Thank you." He turned for the door and glanced at the old man behind the counter, but the man kept his eyes down on the magazine.

They stepped outside and Kim said, "What are you thinking?"

Charlie pulled open the driver's-side door. "Well, I can tell you one thing. She's got a bigger role in all this than she let on. And she sure ain't as dumb as she wanted us to think."

"She's a step ahead of us," Kim said, climbing into the passenger side.

Charlie dialed his phone at the same time he turned the key in the ignition. He held the phone with his hand but used his shoulder at the same time, pressing it against his ear. He backed out of the parking space and turned toward the road. "I'm not sure she ever got on a plane," he said when Frank answered.

"Cab driver give you anything?" Frank said.

"He dropped her off but didn't see her go inside. I have a feeling Roger Flynn was there waiting for her, maybe just doing what they thought would throw us off their scent. A black Mercedes was already there when the cabbie dropped her off at arrivals."

"Arrivals? That son of a bitch... he might've never left Monroe."

"That's what I was wondering. Maybe Jack never got on the plane, had his ex-wife fly it out of there hoping we'd follow... somehow got out of Kim's sight with the bomb scare and all the commotion it caused."

"That would explain why there's no record of him landing anywhere in Florida. Even if he landed on farmland, we'd have something at this point."

"So no sense in us getting a flight just yet," Charlie said, feeling somewhat relieved.

Frank said. "Come back to the office. I'll wait for you. Already got an APB out for Flynn and his Mercedes."

"Assuming he hasn't already abandoned it, got something else," Charlie said.

Chapter 11

Charlie was behind the wheel heading north on US 25 when his phone rang. "Charlie Harlow," he said, without looking at the screen to see who it was. He glanced at Kim watching him from the passenger seat.

"Charlie, it's Stan. Where are you?"

"Where am I?" He looked for a sign ahead. "Just about to hit Twenty-Six, on our way back to Asheville."

"I thought you were catching a flight to Florida?"

"We were," Charlie said. "But it looks like Bella Ray never got on a plane, as we first assumed." He paused a moment. "Frank didn't call you?"

"Not that I'm aware of. But, listen, how far are you from Monroe?"

"Monroe? I'd have to say two, two and a half hours. Why?"

"We have our team at the scene down at Bella Ray Sparrow's house. Brought the dogs today, one of the agents had a hunch... cadaver dog turned up another body, buried under all that rubble."

"In the house?"

"In the basement. Burned beyond recognition. Agents found a couple of empty shells down there, although still too soon to tell if they're a match to the ones used on the other victim."

"How soon you think it'll take to get an ID?" Charlie said as he looked up at the sign for Route 26 toward Asheville.

"This one'll take a little longer. Not much left of him, if it is indeed a male. Only going by the size, so we could be wrong."

"You don't think it's Jack Thornton, do you?" Charlie said.

"I wouldn't make that kind of guess right now. No."

"Well, I would. Think about it, Stan. What if his friend turned on him? What if Jack was one of the friends that invested with him?"

Stan was quiet on the other end. "Charlie? Why don't you let me do my job, I'll let you do yours."

Charlie glanced at Kim, still watching him. "Jesus, Stan. You all right? We're on the same side here, are we not?"

After another brief moment of quiet, Stan said, "I'm sorry. It's just... we've got to go through a process here before we make assumptions like that. State medical examiner's already involved. Got a dental consultant waiting to step in, up in Mecklenburg County."

"It was just a thought," I said.

"Well, it doesn't make any sense. You said yourself he was on that plane. Can't see how within an hour he's barbecued in his girlfriend's basement."

"All right, Stan. I get it. I'll let you do your job. You need anything from me, give me a ring."

Frank stood from his desk as soon as Charlie and Kim walked in the office. "Anything yet from the medical examiner's office?"

Charlie shook his head. "Stan was a little grumpy. I'm not sure I'll be the first one he calls when he gets word."

"What'd you say to him?" Frank said.

Charlie stood in the doorway of Frank's office. "Suggested perhaps the body was Jack Thornton's. Told me to stick to doing my job."

"He's still upset Thornton got away. Can't say I blame him." Frank sat down at his desk. "And he's right. You're not an investigator, Charlie. You come across like a back-seat driver sometimes."

"Is that what he said?"

Frank shook his head. "That's what *I'm* saying." He leaned so he could see out into the office. "Where's Kim?"

She walked up behind Charlie, holding a folder in her hand. "I'm right here."

Charlie stepped into the office and sat in the leather chair across from Frank. Kim leaned against the frame of the door.

Frank gave Kim a nod. "What do *you* think, Kim? You see any way Charlie's correct and there's a chance it's Jack Thornton's body down there in Bella Ray's basement?"

She glanced at Charlie, turned and looked back at her. "I'm sorry, but I agree with Stan. I just don't see how it's possible. A lot would have to happen back there in the time it took him to drive with me to the airport, turn around and—"

"But you said it yourself," Charlie said. "You didn't actually see him get on that airplane. He could've been off in the car, heading back to the house. Got money stashed somewhere…"

"I don't know either," Frank said. "Seems a little far-fetched. I'm going to have to agree with Stan and Kim. Although, no sense in us sitting around until we have confirmation." He had his eyes on Charlie. "So, are we looking for *Jack*? Or Roger?"

"Well, we're assigned with taking Jack Thornton into custody, but that includes any accomplices. I'd say, right now, that includes the other three. So even if we're not sure which one of 'em is dead or alive, we still have a job to do." Frank slid a folder across his desk. "Elizabeth Thornton has associates down in Southwest Florida, in Naples. This came out of Washington, so it's worth looking into."

Charlie grabbed the folder and opened it, looked at the picture of Elizabeth Thornton, older than him by a good few years but quite attractive. "That it? Business associates? Anything else we should know about them?"

"You know what she did for a living?" Frank said.

Charlie flipped through the pages. "Says right here she was a talent scout for modeling agencies?"

Frank nodded. "And you want to guess how Jack met Bella Ray?"

"Through the wife?" Charlie said, looking up from the folder at Frank.

Frank smiled and nodded.

Kim said, "So the ex-wife already knew Bella Ray? Before Jack?"

"Maybe better than Jack," Frank said.

Charlie made a face. "We trying to draw some line from Jack to the ex-wife... to Bella Ray? Can you explain what the significance is the ex knows Bella Ray? We already know they seem to have a whole posse going. And Roger Flynn no longer seems to be just the friend in the background helping his buddy get away."

Charlie's phone rang and he turned the screen toward Frank. "Here he is. Stan the man." He answered. "You still got your panties all bunched up down there?"

"Cut me a break, will you Charlie? You know what? I was supposed to be packing to go away for my anniversary. Wife's ready to divorce me. Here I am dragged into this mess I wasn't—"

"Well, you're going to have to make it up to her," Charlie said. "You don't want to end up like me."

"That's an understatement," Stan said.

Charlie smiled, huffed out a laugh. "So you got anything yet?"

"I do. There was an open safe bolted down in the basement not more than five feet from the body. Door was wide open. Nothing inside, and doesn't look like it was something might've burned up, either."

"Wide open, huh? You sure whatever was in there couldn't have burned?"

"We're sure. It's empty. Remember I told you we found those shells? Well, looks like they're a match to what was used on the farmhand. I'd say the victim in the basement was shot at close range before that house caught on fire."

Charlie pulled the phone from his ear, covered the mic and looked at Frank and Kim. "Found an open safe... shells they picked up match what was used on the farmhand."

Frank said, "Ask him if they've pulled a warrant yet for Roger Flynn's arrest."

Charlie put the phone back to his ear. "Frank wants to know—"

"Yeah, I heard him," Stan said. "We're working on it. Shouldn't be long. I'll call you."

Charlie wasn't sure Stan hung up but looked at the screen and saw that he had. "Stan's having a bad day," Charlie said, shifting his gaze from Frank to Kim. "Wife's about to throw him out."

"You guys marry these women," Frank said, "don't tell 'em what it's really all about. As if they'll sit on their hands for fifty years and think it'll get better." He got up from the desk, shaking his head.

Charlie stood up from the chair and looked at his watch. "I gotta take a drive down to the house, make sure Jennie's all right." He turned to Frank. "Who'd you say's watching her?"

"I told you Foster's got the flu, didn't I?"

Charlie shook his head, making a face of disgust. "No, you didn't. What's that mean?"

Frank glanced at Kim and they both walked out of Frank's office, leaving Charlie behind.

Charlie followed. "Frank? You going to tell me who—"

"Deputy Rivers."

Charlie's eyebrows jumped high on his head, his eyes wide as they'd go. His hands on his hips, he said, "Please tell me you're joking, Frank."

Frank didn't respond, and Charlie knew he was serious as could be.

"Christ, Frank. This is my wife we're talking about."

"Kyle's a fully capable US deputy marshal," Frank said. "He can't spend every day in the courtroom, like he's—"

"I don't want protecting Jennie to be part of his learning curve," Charlie said. "And why *can't* he spend the rest of his career in the courtroom? Plenty of good men..."

"Stop worrying so much," Frank said. "Anything happens, it's on me."

Charlie walked out the door without looking back, let it slam closed behind him and hurried down the hall for the elevator.

Chapter 12

Jennie's car was parked in the driveway when Charlie pulled in behind it. He stepped out with one foot down on the driveway and stood between the car and the open driver's-side door, his arm resting on the roof. He looked over at Kyle Rivers, parked on the road at the front of the house. Charlie closed his door, walked down the end of the driveway and over to the driver's side of Kyle's car.

Kyle rolled down the window and looked up at Charlie.

"Look at you," Charlie said. "Playing with the big boys now, are you? So tell me, what was it brought this about? Someone beg Frank to get you out of the courtroom?"

Kyle looked up at Charlie. "No, Charlie. Not at all. But I want you to know you don't have nothing to worry about. Nothing's gonna happen to Mrs. Harlow under my watch. I promise you."

Charlie leaned with both hands on the top of Kyle's door. "It's easy to be a ballbuster when you have nothing to worry about, hiding in that courtroom. But this here's a much different game now. They don't go through metal detectors before you find yourself face-to-face with the bad guys."

Kyle nodded. "I know that. And I'll say it again... you don't have to worry. I'll keep her safe. You have my word."

Charlie straightened out from the car and looked back toward the house. He turned and looked to the right, down the road. He looked left. "You see anything at all out here? Anybody suspicious driving by?"

"No, Charlie. Nothing at all. It's real quiet out here. I mean, nobody she wasn't expecting, at least."

"Nobody she wasn't *expecting*? What's that supposed to mean, Kyle?"

"Oh, I mean..." Kyle swallowed. "She's had someone here—a couple of times—told me beforehand she'd be expecting a friend."

"Her mother, maybe? Sister?"

Kyle nodded then shook his head, like he wasn't sure how to answer. He swallowed. "It was a man."

Charlie looked back at the house, felt his face turn flush and warm, like the heat of the sun had been turned up. "You know the man's name?"

Kyle shook his head. "No, Charlie. I didn't ask."

"You know you're supposed to know the name of every person who walks within fifty yards of this property? Didn't anybody tell you that?"

Kyle shook his head again, but this time didn't say a word.

Charlie turned from the car and walked up the driveway past his car and up to the front door. He knocked and turned away, his eyes on Kyle out on the road. But Jennie didn't answer, so he knocked again and this time leaned his head into the door when he knocked. "Jennie? It's me, Charlie. You wanna open up?"

The dead bolt popped from the inside and the top lock turned. Jennie pulled open the door with a necklace in her hand. She hung it on her neck and turned her back to Charlie. "You mind helping me with this?"

Charlie looked her up and down from behind, dressed up more than usual, the smell of her sweet perfume stronger than normal. "You going somewhere?" he said, fixing the necklace on her neck under her long hair, down this time.

He followed her into the kitchen and she hadn't answered him. She walked to the stove and, with her back to Charlie, turned a spoon inside the cast iron pot. She reached for a glass of red wine from the counter. "You want a drink?"

Charlie shook his head, looking around the house, noticing it was cleaner, everything a little more straightened out than it normally was. There were flowers on the table. "I was just coming down to check on you, see if everything's all right." He stepped to the window at the front of the house, moved the curtain aside and looked out at Kyle's car out in the road. "Everything okay with Deputy Rivers so far?" He turned from the window.

She nodded. "Seems nice enough, I guess. He's young, isn't he?"

"Oh, but age doesn't mean a thing. He's one of our best," he said, almost biting his tongue as the words came out of his mouth. He didn't want her to worry. "So, Jennie, you didn't answer... you going somewhere?" He nodded toward the stove. "Smells good." He walked from the kitchen and poked his head in the dining room, which they'd only used once or twice while they were married.

The table was set with the fancy china they'd gotten for their wedding—something else they'd rarely used—and one wine glass. He turned back to Jennie, saw her staring back at him.

"Listen, Charlie. I've been meaning to tell you. I mean... I have this friend... I have *a* friend. He's coming over this evening." She held up her hand, the other holding the wine glass. "It's not a big deal. Just dinner. It's—"

"This the same man that young deputy marshal told me's been—"

"Is that what he's doing out there?" She narrowed her eyes. "He just another way for you to keep an eye on me, make sure I don't do anything you don't want me to do? Like have a life of my own?"

"Give me a break, Jennie. You think I'd do that? I'd lose my job if—"

"I don't know if you'd do that or not. I wouldn't put it past you. And, I'll be honest, Charlie... I don't know what to think of you anymore."

Charlie watched her turn from him, grab an apron from the drawer and tie it around her back. She leaned down into the oven, pulled out a pan covered in aluminum foil and place it on top of the stove. She stayed with her back to him.

"Do I know him?" Charlie said.

She shook her head and turned from the stove. "He's just a friend. Someone from work."

"He got a name?"

She held her gaze on Charlie then walked toward him, grabbed him by the arm and pulled him to the door. "His name is Chris. And he's going to be here in ten minutes. I'd appreciate it if you'd... I'd rather not have my husband standing in the kitchen when he shows up." She reached for the door and pulled it open, pushing Charlie toward it.

He didn't put up much of a fight, turning on the concrete landing outside the door to face her. "Just a friend, huh? You're wearing that pretty necklace I gave you... the perfume I used to buy you..." He shook his head and went down the steps. He glanced back at her. "A friend?" He pushed out his best smile, but he didn't think there was much to smile about, looking up at her in the apron he was sure he gave her too, although he remembered she didn't like it much as a Christmas gift. He started along the walk toward his car.

"Charlie?" she said. "You can't keep coming by like this. We're not together anymore. I... I just wish you'd just sign those divorce papers, make things a lot easier on both of us."

He kept walking, stepped around to the driver's side and leaned on the hot roof. "I'll try to remember," he said. He pulled open the door and looked back at her. "I'm just making sure you're all right, Jennie. I'll always worry about you."

She looked out toward the street at Kyle, watching them but looking away when she caught his eyes. "Charlie, is it really necessary he's out here? I don't see how someone'd come after me. Most men wouldn't object to it if someone did."

"You mean someone going after my wife?" He grinned at her and stepped into the car. He closed the door and put down the passenger window, leaning over the seat so he could see her up on the top of the step. "When we catch Hunter King, we'll all leave you alone. Okay? Until then, it helps me sleep at night knowing you're not down here all alone."

Jennie gave him a smile, her red lips pressed together. She walked into the house.

Charlie watched her close the door. He shifted his car into reverse. He pulled out onto the road and stopped next to Kyle Rivers. He waited for Kyle to put the passenger window down. "Her friend's still here past midnight, do me a favor and let me know." Charlie started to pull away then stopped, backed up again and waited for Kyle to put down his window one more time. "Forget I just said that," he said, shaking his head. "That's not part of your job."

Chapter 13

THE OFFICE WAS QUIET other than a couple of deputy marshals in their cubicles tapping their keyboards. Charlie walked to his desk, still tired from getting up earlier than he normally did and without much more than a few hours sleep the past few nights.

Charlie wasn't much in the mood for talking, knowing he had little time before the North Carolina Bureau of Investigations were sending over the internal investigator to interview him about shooting Gunner King, the man who'd allegedly killed Deputy Ted Moore with a weapon nobody had been able to locate.

Charlie filled a cup with coffee and went to his office. He took a sip and picked up a folder someone had left on his desk with a sticky note on top that said *Roger Flynn*. He recognized Kim's handwriting and opened the folder. He glanced over the first page, an old court filing from fifteen years earlier when Roger's wife had been killed in a boating accident. Roger collected a million dollars from the life insurance policy, which of course raised a red flag, and the police dug up enough—or so they thought—to say Roger had been the one who killed her.

But he was never convicted.

Charlie looked at his watch. It was seven twenty. He pulled his phone from his pocket and called Kim. "You awake?" he said as soon as she answered.

"I am now."

"You always sleep this late?" he said, having fun with her.

She yawned into the phone. "I was at the office till two."

Charlie put the folder on the desk. "I was just looking over the court filing you left me."

"I decided to dig a little deeper into Roger Flynn. You read it?"

"Yeah, I read it," Charlie said. "Most of it. You think maybe he got away with killing his wife?"

"You see who was on the boat with him when she went overboard?" Kim said.

"I guess I didn't read enough of it." He opened the folder on his desk but he had a feeling he knew where Kim was going. "Jack Thornton?"

"I'm sure the FBI knows all about it. But it was news to me."

"News to me too," Charlie said. "So looks like these two go back a ways." He flipped through the pages.

Kim said, "That body down in the basement turns out to be Jack's and it's determined Roger's the one who killed him..."

"Outside of taking whatever money was in that safe, maybe Flynn was sick of worrying Jack would talk? Especially if he was afraid they'd make some kind of deal with him."

"You see the second page?" Kim said.

Charlie flipped the paper. "What are these? Flynn's bank statements?"

"Took all his money out a few weeks back, although it didn't add up to much. He was broke."

Charlie looked at all the money the guy had in the bank at one time not too long ago. "I'd like that amount to be my *broke*," he said.

"Well, for someone who had a few million a little over a year ago..."

Charlie said, "So there's a big pile of cash somewhere."

One of the other deputies walked over to Charlie's office and knocked on the frame of his door. "Charlie, good-looking woman from BOI's here to see you."

Charlie gave him a look and nodded, walked around his desk and stepped to the door so he could see the front of the office.

A woman, tall and pretty with a serious look on her face, caught his eye as soon as he looked and smiled, although not the friendly kind Charlie would have preferred.

"Kim," he said. "I gotta run. Agent from the Bureau of Investigations is here. I'll see you when you get here." He walked from his office toward the woman, extending his hand as he approached her. "Deputy Harlow," he said.

She reached out to shake his hand. "Gina Williams, North Carolina Bureau of Investigations." She looked around the office. "Can we use the conference room?"

"Yes, of course," he said, and gestured for her to walk ahead of him. He pointed. "Right in there."

She didn't hesitate to take a seat at the end of the long conference-room table. She placed her briefcase on the table and popped it open, removed a folder and a digital recording device. She closed the top and put the briefcase on the floor.

Charlie stood over the table, trying to get a look at the paperwork in front of her. "Can I get you a coffee? Or tea?"

She seemed pleasant enough, he thought.

"No, thank you. I'm okay right now." She held up the bottle of water she already had in front of her, cracked the top and took a sip. "If we can just get started..." Gina Williams gave him a smirk and looked down in her folder. "This conversation will be recorded." She looked up at him. "You do understand?"

"Yes ma'am," he said. He pulled the chair out across from her. "So that you may use it for quality and training purposes?"

She glanced at him and held her gaze.

Not amused.

Charlie sat down and tried to get comfortable, pushed himself back from the table and crossed one leg on top of the other. But it didn't feel right, like he was trying to hard to appear relaxed. He put both feet on the ground and rolled the chair closer, his stomach up against the table. He folded his hands and watched her flip through the papers, getting things in order, using the pen in her hand to run down whatever it was she was looking at.

After a few moments she closed the folder, and from underneath it produced a white pad, lined. She clicked the top of her pen, reached for the recorder and pressed the red button. "Okay," she said. "Let's begin."

Charlie swallowed.

She removed the cap from her plastic bottle of water and took a sip, replaced the cap and gave Charlie a nod. "Why don't you start from the beginning, with as much detail as you can."

"Where do you want me to start?"

"However the day started."

"You mean, I got up and used the bathroom, brushed my teeth..."

She had the pen in her hand on top of the white pad, her eyes down. "If that's how you want to get started."

Charlie nodded, although she wasn't looking at him.

She was all business.

"I got in here around seven that morning, left about twenty minutes later to meet Deputy Moore in Candler, just outside the Hillside Mobile Home park. The second deputy, name was Jay Totum, was there with us. Although I got the feeling he was there more for the ride... uniform too big for him, like a kid in a suit going to his first dance. You know what I mean?"

Gina lifted her eyes from the paper and glanced at Charlie. "Go ahead." But she held up her index finger. "Weren't you supposed to wait for Deputy Marshal Kim Riggins before you left to meet the deputies?"

Charlie shook his head. "Well, not initially. Deputy Moore and me... we weren't too concerned. Serve the warrant, get Gunner King in the car and be on our way. Wasn't the first time for either of us."

"But just so I'm clear and we have it on the record, the original plan was to wait for Deputy Marshal Riggins?"

Charlie hesitated a moment, eyeballed the recorder and thought it through, knew he had to make sure everything he said came out the way it was supposed to. "Yes, ma'am."

"Yes, you were supposed to wait for her?" She gazed at Charlie.

"Yes. We were both supposed to go together with both deputies from the Buncombe County Sheriff's Office." He tried to look at what she was putting on the paper, but the letters she formed were too small. Even if he stood right over her, he wasn't sure he'd know what she wrote.

"I'm sorry," she said. "Please continue." She picked up the recorder and looked it over, placed it back on the table a little closer to Charlie.

"I knocked, announced who we were and why we were there. Told him we had a warrant for Gunner King's arrest."

"But I'm sure you were aware there was a chance someone could be on the other side of the door with a weapon, were you not?"

Charlie pushed himself back from the table, kept his hands folded in front of him. "We are always aware the person on the other side of a door may have a weapon. At no point did I let my guard down, if that's what you're asking?"

She looked up from her notes. "Was your gun holstered?"

"Yes, it was. But that doesn't mean I wasn't prepared."

She made another note. "That's not why I asked. I don't doubt you were prepared. I'm asking if you used proper caution, the way you've been trained?"

Charlie folded his arms at his chest. "Is that a serious question?"

She looked at him, as if waiting for his answer, but likely didn't appreciate his response. "I always use caution and proper judgment."

She put the pen down on the pad and straightened out in her chair. "You've been in this situation before," she said. "And I get the feeling—and I'm not the only one—you leave your weapon in your holster on purpose, like you think you're in the wild west. Is that something that may describe the way you—"

"You can think whatever you want. But I didn't pull that trigger until after I was fired upon."

When Mr. King had his back to you?"

"His back to me? He fired a shot."

"There was no sign of the weapon, or that he was the one who fired it. The weapon has yet to be recovered, is that correct?"

Charlie ran his tongue inside his cheek, looked away and out toward the window overlooking downtown Asheville. "He killed that deputy... a good man. I'm just not sure I understand why we're even here."

"This isn't the first time you've killed a man."

Charlie held his gaze on her for a moment and nodded. "It's not like any of 'em were good people. I can tell you that much. And everything I've done—everything I do—is always by the book."

That last part wasn't exactly true, but it was something he knew he had to put out there.

"What do you believe happened to the weapon used to kill Deputy Edward Moore?"

"Teddy," he said. "We called him Teddy. Or Ted." He shrugged. "I assume you have the report... you have it somewhere in your notes. A shot was fired at me. Now, I ducked, of course. I came up and fired."

"You didn't see the weapon?"

"Did I see it?" Charlie took a moment. "You know that answer."

"You fired a weapon at a man you're not sure had fired at you."

Charlie laughed. "Maybe you oughta talk to someone at the sheriff's office, because there was no doubt in anyone's mind which direction it was fired from."

"But you didn't see him pull the trigger?"

"I told you, I—"

"Yes or no, Deputy Harlow. Did you see him pull the trigger?"

Charlie scratched his cheek and shook his head. "No." He rolled the chair back and stood up. "You mind I grab a coffee?"

"It'll just be a few more—"

Charlie held up his finger. "I'm sorry. I really need some coffee." He didn't wait for her to respond, pulled open the door and walked out into the office shaking his head. He turned into the kitchen and Frank was in there with his jacket on, pouring himself a mug of coffee.

"Everything all right in there?" Frank said.

"Oh, it's wonderful," Charlie said, taking a white Styrofoam cup from the stack next to the coffee machine.

"Well that's good to hear. When you're done I need to talk to you and Kim, if she's around yet?"

"Not yet, I don't think."

"Well, when you're done and Kim gets in, we need to talk about Roger Flynn." Frank turned and walked out of the kitchen.

Charlie poured a coffee and leaned against the counter in front of the sink. He took a sip, not interested in going back in that conference room right away. But he knew he had to, and walked back in and again sat down across from her. He sipped his coffee. "You mentioned we were almost done?"

She reached for the recorder and pushed the button. The green light came on the side. "Let's back up a little, to when you knocked on the door."

"Gunner didn't answer the door. They rarely do on the first knock, unless it's an unsuspecting significant other who hadn't been warned. Or sometimes they're just too dumb to think we'd ever find them."

"Deputy Moore kicked in the door?"

Charlie cracked a slight smile and nodded. He'd always liked Ted. "Teddy had these big feet, size thirteen or fourteen, I think. All I had to do was give him a nod and he knew it was up to him to get the door open. You didn't need a battering ram with Teddy around. I mean, not on a mobile home's door anyway. But, well... you get my point."

Gina Williams had her head down, taking notes.

Charlie continued, "But Teddy's foot had barely touched the door when the shot was fired." He paused a moment, looking down at his coffee. "Sent poor Teddy stumbling back. Goddamn chest exploded... man didn't have a chance." Charlie had his fingers around the cup in front of him.

Gina Williams said, "And then you entered the home?"

"I knew Teddy was dead, without a doubt." He nodded. "Deputy Totum, got some Indian in him I think, was by his side, but I'm not sure he knew which end was up. Kid couldn't even work his two-way the way he was shaking... white as a ghost like he was going to lose his cookies."

"And you told him to stop?"

"Told *who* to stop? Gunner?" Charlie nodded, not sure it mattered if he did or not. "Of course I told him to stop. More than once. Even after he fired that shot."

"But, again, you don't know if he's the one who fired it. According to the report he was at least one hundred yards away and—"

"Oh, he wasn't a hundred yards away. I mean, by the time I fired back at him he was. Give or take twenty-five yards or so. The son of a bitch was fast; ran another twenty-five or so yards before I had my gun raised."

Chapter 14

CHARLIE LOOKED UP AT the clock behind the bar at The Coyote Grille, sipping bourbon, watching Lindsey on the other side counting the drawer. It was twelve forty-seven in the morning.

Other than the TV and two men being a bit loud down the far end of the bar, the place was empty.

Lindsey had already given last call when Charlie turned and looked at the men. One of them—the skinny one—held up his glass and looked into it with one eye closed. Whatever was still inside dripped onto his face.

"Hey sweetie," the man said, his words tangled in his tongue. "Can we get two more?"

Lindsey was in the middle of counting cash, acted like she hadn't heard the man. She wrote some numbers down on a cocktail napkin and slipped it under the cash register drawer. She brushed her hair back on her head and closed the drawer. She started toward him. "Sorry, hon. I already gave you last call. Register's closed."

The other man, thick-bearded with a green John Deere cap on his head spoke up, the same swollen tongue as his friend, "I didn't hear you say *last call*. So why don't you just give us two more and we'll call it even." He smiled, one eye practically closed. "We won't tell no one."

Lindsey chose to ignore them. She opened the dishwasher behind the bar and steam rose up around her. She reached in and took out a couple of clean pint glasses and stacked them upside down on the red rubber mat by the tap on the back of the bar. "All right, you two. Time to go home. I gotta lock the door."

Charlie sat, quiet, a crack of a smile as he looked into his glass. He had a feeling he knew where this might be going. And he was in a mood.

"Hey, why you being like that?" the skinny one said. "Don't make me climb over this bar and get it myself."

His friend laughed. They *both* laughed.

"She already said it was last call," Charlie said, his eyes still down on his drink. "You're too drunk to hear it, that's your problem." He turned his gaze to the two men. "Now why don't you two boys get on out of here. Time to hit the road." Charlie tossed back the last sip of Jack Daniels and pushed the glass forward.

Lindsey gave him a look, shaking her head. "Charlie, don't..."

Charlie didn't move. He didn't get up from the stool but turned and watched as both men came toward him. "I don't recommend you take another step in my direction," he said, "if you know what's good for you."

The heavier one with the thick beard and the John Deere hat took a step anyway, his skinny friend right behind him. He lifted his dirty T-shirt and showed Charlie the .38 tucked in his pants. "What're you gonna do, tough guy?"

Charlie held out his hand, his index finger extended. "Hold up," he said. "Let me show you something." He pulled out his wallet and extended his arm, flashing the gold badge with *United States Marshal* etched on the circle around the five-point star. "Sir, I'm a deputy U.S. Marshal, and I suggest before you even think about removing that gun from your pants, you take a moment to reconsider."

The bearded man turned and looked over his shoulder at his friend. He put his hand out, like he was holding his friend back, and took another step toward Charlie.

"I'm warning you," Charlie said. He got up from the stool. "Take one more step."

"Boys!" Lindsey yelled.

The burly one with the John Deere hat raised his hand to throw a punch at Charlie.

But Charlie saw it coming at him, caught the man's hand and twisted it, had the man turned around with his arm as far as it would go up behind his back. Charlie grabbed his other arm and slammed his face down on the bar. He held him there and got close to his ear. "I only got one good ear, so I understand if maybe you're hard of hearing." He reached down and around the front of the man's pants, removed the .38 and slid it along the bar away from them. "Put that somewhere," Charlie said to Lindsey.

The man grunted and tried to get loose, but Charlie wasn't letting go.

But the skinny one was free and pulled a gun of his own, lunged at Charlie with it pointed at him.

Charlie stepped out of the way and grabbed the skinny one's arm and a shot went off and into the ceiling. The light over their heads blew out and shattered bits of glass fell on top of them.

The big man was free now and up on his feet. He threw a punch at Charlie but froze when he saw the barrel of a shotgun pointed toward his face, Lindsey on the other end of it from behind the bar.

"You get your ass out of here," she said. "I ever see either one of you in here again..."

Charlie cracked a crooked smile looking at the two men's faces, the skinny one shaking like he'd never seen the barrel of a shotgun that close to his eyeball before.

They both turned for the door, Charlie watching with his hand on the Glock holstered on his hip. The last thing he wanted was to pull it out and have to use it on a couple of idiots from the mountains... especially knowing he was one minor incident away from working the courtrooms for the rest of his career.

He pushed open the door and stood on the deck watching the two men stumble through the parking lot. He yelled down to them, "She works a long and hard day, likes to close on time so she can get some rest. Hope there's no hard feelings."

The skinny one turned and yelled something up at Charlie, but Charlie didn't know what he'd said, turned and walked back inside. He pulled the door closed behind him and turned the lock.

Lindsey was looking up at the ceiling. "Hope that didn't hit my bed." She filled Charlie's glass with a good pour of Jack and grabbed her own glass, filled it just as much and threw the whole thing back.

Charlie opened his eyes, turned and looked at Lindsey, sound asleep, a little buzz coming from inside her throat. He sat up and tried to look outside through the window but couldn't see a thing. It was hard to tell if it was light or dark out with the type of curtains she had hanging from the rod.

He sat up in the darkness, the only light coming from the clock next to Lindsey.

It was four thirty-eight.

He hung his feet off the edge of the bed and stood up. He leaned over and picked up his pants from the floor, slipped them on and felt around for his watch on the nightstand next to the bed. In doing so, he knocked over the glass he'd carried up from the bar downstairs but grabbed it before it fell to the floor. He put his watch on his wrist and reached into his pants pocket for his phone. He checked, saw he'd missed a text from Stan Cooper not ten minutes earlier. Maybe that's what woke him up. He wasn't sure.

The text read:

Body ID'd. Jack Thornton.

"Jesus," Charlie said, under his breath. He had a good feeling it was going to be, but nobody believed it. There was another side of him that couldn't see how it could've been possible. He leaned over and grabbed his boots, sat back on the edge of the bed and pulled them on, tied them both tight and headed out the door.

He stood outside on the deck just outside Lindsey's apartment on the third floor above the bar. He knew it was too early and maybe Frank had already talked to Stan. But Charlie called him anyway. The phone rang three times and stopped on the fourth when Frank answered. Charlie could hear the muffled sounds on the other end, like Frank had gotten tangled up in the sheets trying to answer.

"This'd better be good," Frank said.

"Sorry to mess up your much-needed beauty rest, but I got a text from Stan a few minutes ago. That body's been identified. It's Jack Thornton."

Frank was silent. "Jack Thornton? The charred body in the basement?"

"Yup."

Charlie continued down the wood stairs down the back of the building, onto the deck off the bar and down another flight to the parking lot. He pulled his keys from his pants and opened the door, the phone still up to his ear.

"Where are you?" Frank said.

"Just getting in my car." Charlie ducked his head into the driver's seat.

"Where you going, the office?"

Charlie turned the key in the ignition and looked up at the sign, *Coyote Grille*. "Yeah. I just gotta make a quick stop first." He put the car in drive but slapped it back into park. "Shit. Forgot my wallet upstairs." He stepped out with the engine still running.

"Upstairs? Where are you?"

Charlie had kept whatever was going on with him and Lindsey quiet, although he knew Frank had a good idea something was up. He went back up the stairs, crossed the deck and jogged up another flight to Lindsey's apartment. He stood outside her door and said to Frank, "Will I see you at the office?"

Before Frank had a chance to answer, the dark morning was filled with a blinding flash of light and a deafening explosion that almost knocked Charlie off his feet. His hand tore through the screen on the aluminum door as he jumped back, fell against the railing behind him.

He pushed himself back up to his feet and looked down at the parking lot, could almost feel the heat coming off the twenty-foot flames and black smoke pouring from his Crown Victoria toppled on its side and up against a tree, burning.

His phone was on the top step and he reached down, put it up to his ear. "Frank?"

The door to Lindsey's apartment over the bar opened and she stood in the doorway, staring out at Charlie. She took a step outside and wrapped her arms around him. "Charlie, I didn't know if you were—"

"You all right?" he said.

She nodded. "Are you?"

"Yeah, I'm all right." He turned and looked down toward the parking lot. "But looks like I'm going to need another car."

Chapter 15

The fire department, Asheville police, and rescue vehicles took up most of the dirt parking lot outside Coyote Grille. Frank and Kim stood with Charlie talking to the three officers, two from Asheville PD's Hazardous Device Team.

Charlie described the two men he'd had a run-in with to the officers, although he told them neither looked smart enough to know how to plant a bomb, never mind knowing how to make it work so it'd go off once the engine warmed to a certain degree.

Frank had a look on his face with a crooked smile, maybe even winked at one of the officers. "There's a long list of people who'd like Deputy Harlow dead. So we can just add two more to the list."

"What if it was Roger Flynn?" Kim said, turning to Frank and Charlie.

Charlie said, "There's a big difference between emptying containers of gas on a house and getting a bomb to tick the right way."

Frank looked at Charlie and shook his head. "All you gotta know is someone who knows how to do it. I wouldn't count out Roger Flynn just yet."

Kim followed the two officers toward Charlie's car. Or at least what was left of it.

Frank looked up at Lindsey, watching them from the other side of the railing, up on the deck outside the bar. She had a cigarette in her mouth. "So how long's this been going on?" he said, turning his eyes to Charlie.

"*This*? What's *this*?"

Frank laughed. "Don't play me for a fool, Charlie. You know what I'm talking about." He looked up again. "Between you and Lindsey."

Charlie shook his head. "There's nothing going on. I just crashed here, had a couple extra drinks and she talked me out of driving."

Frank held his gaze on Charlie, but Charlie turned away, started toward his blackened vehicle.

"Too many drinks, huh?" Frank followed after him, shaking his head. "I wasn't born yesterday, you know."

Charlie looked back at him. "That is a fact, Frank. You were not born yesterday." He grinned, and stopped where Kim and the Asheville Police officers stood, looking the car over.

Kim had her arms folded, watching, but not doing much else. "They've located the device," she said, glancing back at Charlie. "Believe it or not, the agent over there said it looks to be the type of bomb that should've gone off as soon as you turned over the ignition."

Charlie was surprised, scratched the side of his head and looked around the parking lot. "I could see those two boys out here waiting for me with a couple of two-by-fours. Or maybe bust up my windows with a baseball bat. But, I just can't see—" His phone rang and he looked at the screen. "It's Stan. Let me grab this." He answered. "Stan, hey I—"

"Oh, good. You're alive?" Stan said.

"Guess you heard what happened?"

"Yeah, of course I heard. FBI got the call; wasn't sure I was going to have to head up there and get involved myself. I hear it might've been a couple of rednecks you pissed off at a bar up there?"

"Where the hell'd you hear that? I mean, the part about me pissing off a couple of rednecks is true. But I'm not buying it was them who blew up my car. Already found the device, so it was planned ahead."

"Asheville PD's investigating?"

"They are, yes. But more importantly... I got your text. I was on the phone with Frank when the car blew up."

"Do you need me to admit you were right?" Frank said.

Charlie looked around the parking lot. "You just did. And I appreciate that." He grinned into the phone. "You able to piece any of it together yet?"

"Spoke to Carl over at the medical examiner's office... Jack had been shot at close range... the shells were from a 12-Gauge. Must've left him there, burned the house down to cover it up."

"A lot to cover up a dead body. And unsuccessfully, to boot," Charlie said. "Roger Flynn the prime suspect?"

"I just got word; footage at that gas station shows it was him filling up those containers."

"Wonder what Bella Ray Sparrow knew about it. Was probably planned before we showed up."

"Well, we don't know anything for sure at this point. But I have a hard time believing she wasn't somehow involved with Roger Flynn from the beginning."

"The way I see it," Charlie said, "is the ex-wife is in on taking Jack down—maybe even has something going on with Roger herself—flies the plane out of that airport just to throw us off their track. Roger takes Jack back to the house, makes him open that safe and finishes him off. Whether he got what he was looking for or not."

Charlie looked up at Lindsey, sitting at the top of the stairs to her apartment over the bar, still in her long T-shirt, nothing on her feet. "Gotta run, Stan. I'll catch up with you in a little bit." He walked over to Lindsey, smoking her cigarette and talking to the officers, trying to answer questions.

She glanced at Charlie and smiled, a straight line between her lips.

"And besides those two men," one officer said, "is there anyone else you can think of may've looked suspicious... maybe had an eye toward Charlie?"

Lindsey stayed quiet, her eyes down toward the deck's floor beneath her red-painted toenails. She looked at Charlie, then back at the officer. "There was a woman... came in and had a couple of drinks." She glanced up at Charlie. "All the women look at him, of course. But this particular one, I don't know, she seemed to've had a hard time keeping her eyes off him."

Charlie rolled his eyes and turned away, looking down toward the parking lot.

The officer said to Charlie, "Any idea who she's referring to?"

Charlie shook his head.

"I didn't say she wasn't seated at the bar," Lindsey said. She turned to the officer. "Charlie had his back to her. She was seated at one of the high-top tables under the Elvis Presley painting, to the left of the door."

The officer said, "And you never saw this woman before?"

Lindsey shook her head. "No."

Charlie said, "Why would whoever blew up my car go in the bar? Could've just as easily kept an eye on me from out here, if that's what you're thinking." He straightened his hat on his head.

The officer held his pad in his hand, the tip of the pen resting on the paper. He looked down at Lindsey. "Can you describe her?"

"Well, she was pretty. Older than me and Charlie."

Charlie looked at her, wasn't exactly sure how old Lindsey was, but younger than him by a handful of years. He said, "How *much* older?"

Lindsey shrugged and held her gaze on Charlie, like she was thinking. "I'm surprised you hadn't noticed her, Charlie. You seem to notice everything." She took a drag from her cigarette.

Charlie turned away from the smoke rising up toward him and turned his face. He hated the smell. Might've been the only thing he didn't like about Lindsey.

"She had those glasses over her eyes, you know, the ones pilots wear." Lindsey used her hands and held them near her eyes to show how big they were.

"Aviator glasses?" Charlie said.

Lindsey nodded.

Charlie looked at the officer. "I don't know what to tell you. I'm willing to guess the woman had nothing to do with any of this. Just stopping off for a quiet drink at The Coyote Grille."

The officer held his gaze on Charlie for a moment. "All right, I get it. But it's better than anything else we have right now." He turned back to Lindsey. "How old would you say this woman was?"

Lindsey shrugged. "I don't know. Without seeing her eyes, it was hard to tell. Maybe somewhere in her late fifties? I could see it around her mouth and chin. Did I already say she had short hair? And I mean, real short. Almost buzzed."

The officer continued with his notes, writing on the small pad. "Dark hair?" he said. "Would you say it was black?"

Lindsey nodded.

Charlie held his gaze on her, thinking. "How'd she pay?" he said. "Credit card?"

"Cash," Lindsey said. "Left a decent tip, too."

Charlie started for the stairs. "I'll let you two finish up. I'm going to go see if they found anything else down there, around my car." He turned back to Lindsey. "If Kim can't give me a ride back, is it all right I borrow your car?"

Chapter 16

CHARLIE AND FRANK WALKED in the office together, went straight to Kim's cubicle where she stood with eight-by-ten photographs spread on her desk, one of them in her hand.

"Bella Ray?" Charlie said, looking over Kim's shoulder. He knew who it was her right away, even with the baseball cap and dark glasses on her face. "Where were they?"

"A train stop in Charlotte," Kim said. She picked up another photo from the desk and handed it to Frank. "We believe the woman next to her is Jack Thornton's wife," she said. "She looks different... hair's a lot shorter." She handed it to Charlie.

His eyes were fixed on the photo of the attractive older woman with jet-black hair, chopped short with the aviator glasses on her face. He looked up at Frank and Kim. "This is who Lindsey described at the bar. I didn't know she'd chopped off her hair."

"And colored it," Kim said.

Frank said, "Are you telling me Lindsey saw her at the bar? You didn't say—"

"She was at the high-top table along the wall. You know the Elvis poster? She sat under it. Watching me, I guess."

Kim said, "You're saying Liz Thornton put that bomb in your car?"

"I'm saying the description Lindsey gave the police matches this photo." He held up the eight-by-ten and took a photo of it with his phone, handed the picture back to Kim and tapped the screen, sent it with a text to Lindsey:

This the woman you saw?

"You didn't see her yourself?" Kim said.

Charlie shook his head. "I'm not into short hair." He smiled, looked down at his screen and turned it so Frank and Kim could see Lindsey's reply:

Yes!

Charlie shook his head and ran his hand through his hair, left it there for a moment holding it back. "Jesus," he said. "She was right there in front of me."

"Behind you," Frank said, "Which is odd, because it's not like you to sit with your back to the door, not notice someone right behind you. But maybe you hadn't had your eyes on the pretty bartender, you might've noticed her." He cracked a slight smile. "Let's just get tracking these two ladies before we miss them again."

"No photos of Flynn?" Charlie said. He shuffled the photos around on the desk and looked up at Kim. "When did you say this was taken?"

"This morning, came in from Charlotte Meck PD... showed up on their city-wide monitoring system from the cameras at a train station on South Boulevard. It's the local commuter rail... the LYNX."

"This isn't Amtrak?" Frank said.

Charlie said, "Could've taken the LYNX downtown, grabbed a cab or Uber and over to the Amtrak station. It's on Tryon."

"There's a reason they're in the Charlotte area," Kim said. "Something brought them back."

Frank gave Charlie one of his looks, maybe annoyed, shaking his head. "We need to get ahead of these folks. We're never gonna catch them if we're always a step behind."

"Well, they drove all the way out here," Charlie said. "Took the time to blow up my car."

"I don't think it was just the car they were trying to blow up," Frank said. "They see you as an obstacle, they must've believed it was something needed to be taken care of." He turned to Kim. "Might be smart... make sure you don't leave your Tahoe parked on the road, or somewhere out of your sight." He turned and started to walk toward his office.

Charlie said, "Frank?"

Frank stopped and looked back, his eyes narrowed. "Charlie?"

"This doesn't make sense. First Bella Ray's on a bus leaving South Carolina. We thought she was on a plane, but we don't know. Now she's in Charlotte?"

Frank said, "It's not our job to make sense of everything. We have warrants for each of their arrests now. All we gotta be worried about is getting them in custody."

"I know that, Frank. I'm just saying, what if they know they're being watched." He looked at the photo again. "Almost looks to me they knew that camera was there."

"Like part of what they're doing is to throw us off their trail?" Frank said.

Charlie shrugged. "Maybe. Even, if you look at what happened to my car… I'm just not sure it all makes a lot of sense." He walked by Frank and into the meeting room, looked at the full map of a good part of the Southeast, most of it North and South Carolina and into Georgia. He called out toward the doorway, "Kim, got a second?"

He stared at the map and looked back as Kim walked in behind him. He pointed at Charlotte. "They were here yesterday." He ran his finger up 321, then to the left along Route 40. "Made it out to Asheville last night, which I assume was by car."

Frank stood in the doorway. "We'll have to assume the three of them are still together. But we don't know for sure." He walked toward the map and stood next to Charlie, moved a pin and stuck it in where the Coyote Grille was located. "I agree with you, Charlie. Don't make much sense. Unless they're heading somewhere west of here?"

"And maybe they're just going to keep going," Kim said, standing on the other side of Charlie now.

Charlie looked at her, on his right, then back to Frank on his left. "We know where any of 'em grew up? Including Jack Thornton? I can't help but think they're looking for something belonged to Jack, whether it's money or—"

"Bella Ray, we already know's from Monroe," Kim said.

Frank gave a nod. "I believe Liz Thornton's a native Floridian. Jack Thornton was born in Tennessee. Oak Ridge, I believe. Roger Flynn might be from around the same area."

Charlie stepped back from the map, his hands on his hips. "So they stopped off in Asheville, get me out of the picture—or so they'd hoped—maybe head west for whatever it is they're looking for? Oak Ridge?" Charlie looked at his watch. "We can be out that way in about two, two and a half hours. Maybe contact the locals, give 'em a heads-up."

"On a hunch?" Kim said. "Are you serious?"

"You got a better idea?"

Kim and Frank exchanged a look and Frank shrugged.

Kim said, "Leave from here? Right now?"

Charlie nodded. "I don't see why not. We're already behind by half a day, at least. Another twenty-four hours, who knows where they'll be..."

Frank was quiet, his arms crossed in front of his chest but one hand up on his chin. "You know, I'm just not sure it makes sense, have you two driving up and down the whole Southeast looking for—"

"Actually, going east and west now." He grinned at Frank.

But Frank didn't appear to be in the mood for Charlie, the smart-ass. "You have no idea if they're out in Oak Ridge or even anywhere in Tennessee, Charlie." He glanced at the map. "Be better off throwing a dart at this thing." Frank followed Charlie out from the room. "I'm serious, Charlie. We don't have the resources to keep running around just because you got some feeling in your gut." He looked back at Kim, still standing in front of the map, looking it over. "He know he doesn't even have a vehicle to drive right now?"

Charlie stopped and spoke past Frank to Kim. "You mind driving?"

She stepped through the doorway. "You know I prefer being behind the wheel over being a passenger in your car."

"You saying you don't like my driving?"

"I'm saying I don't mind driving."

Charlie said, "All right, let's pull together a list of relatives out there. Of both Jack and Roger. Their brothers, sisters, sisters' uncles' cousins… let's get every name of every single relative within fifty miles of Oak Ridge." Charlie went into his office, came out with his bulletproof vest in his hand, his Glock still in the holster, and a hardshell case carrying a Remington 870 he'd been okayed to use from his time spent in the Special Operations Unit.

Frank watched him and put his hand over his face. "This is it, Charlie. Last chance. You don't come back with all three in custody…" He turned and walked into his office without finishing his thought.

Charlie walked toward him and stood in the doorway. "Who do you know over there," he said. "What is that over there, Anderson County? Is that right?"

Frank sat at his desk and picked up his phone. "I'm calling the sheriff's office right now, let them know you're on your way."

"What about the Oak Ridge Police Department?"

Frank gave him a look, like he'd had enough of Charlie trying to run the show. "Would you give me a damn minute? Anything else you need me to do for you, Charlie? Maybe get you a cup of coffee? Massage your feet?" He pointed toward the door with the phone in his hand. "Now will you please get out of my office? And close the door."

Chapter 17

Kim drove at a pretty good clip and made it out to Clinton, Tennessee in just a few minutes over two hours. She pulled into the parking lot of the Anderson County Sheriff's Office, off Broad Street.

Charlie was in the passenger seat looking over notes on a small pad with the spiral-wire binding on top. He reached for the handle on the passenger door and said, "First stop's about twenty minutes, door-to-door."

Charlie and Kim both stepped from the Tahoe, being watched from the stairs by a tall and thin sheriff with muscles he appeared to want to show off, the way he had his shirtsleeves rolled halfway up his biceps.

"Charlie?" he said, extending his hand. "Sheriff Dale Jones."

Charlie shook the sheriff's hand and nodded. He turned to Kim. "This is Deputy U.S. Marshal Kim Riggins."

Kim shook the sheriff's hand.

Sheriff Jones said, "Frank said you got three warrants; been a bit of a challenge getting them served?"

Charlie nodded. "You could say that." He pulled up the waist of his pants behind him and looked around at the building. "This the county courthouse, or..."

"Juvenile court," the deputy said, looking back toward the door he stood in front of.

Charlie said, "About a week ago we were down in Monroe, North Carolina—just below Charlotte—turned out this particular man was shot and killed by his so-called friends. Burned him down with his girlfriend's house."

Sheriff Jones raised his eyebrows and removed his hat, scratching the top of his head. "Tell me if I have this straight, the way Frank explained it... the girlfriend and the ex-wife of the deceased fugitive are on the run together with the dead man's best friend?"

"That's about right," Charlie said. "Roger Flynn is with the two women: Elizabeth Thornton, the ex-wife, and Bella Ray Sparrow—she's the girlfriend."

"Of the deceased?"

Charlie nodded.

"So what makes you sure they're here in Anderson County?"

"Well..." Charlie hesitated. He wasn't going to tell the sheriff he wasn't sure, although that was nothing but the truth. "We traced them from Charlotte early yesterday, know they made it out to Asheville late at night. Turns out Roger Flynn and Jack Thornton have relatives out this way. Both were born in Oak Ridge."

"They blew up your car?" the sheriff said.

"Frank told you that?"

The sheriff shook his head. "No, just heard about it."

Charlie and Kim exchanged a quick glance.

Charlie said, "Had the ex-wife sitting five feet away at a place called The Coyote Grille the night before it happened. So, as you can imagine, I'm a bit anxious about getting my hands on them."

The sheriff's face got somewhat twisted, a slight snarl to his lip. "You knew she was there?"

Charlie didn't need to get into the details. He handed a folded piece of paper to the sheriff. "This here's a list of relatives. I don't know how many deputies you have who're able to help, but—"

Sheriff Jones nodded, "I got three waiting inside, wrapping up a couple things. I can have them on this; give me about twenty minutes?"

Charlie nodded. "I marked the names on the list for your deputies to focus on."

The sheriff looked over the paper, ran his finger down the list and looked up at Charlie. "Whatever you need, just say the word. You're in charge here."

Kim looked out toward the road. "What about the airport? Closest one is Oliver Springs?"

Sheriff Jones nodded. "Yes, it is."

Charlie said, "You got any men out that way already, by any chance?"

"Generally, that's a quiet area out there around the airport. They've got a couple private security guards... I believe one TSA agent who may only be there part time. Otherwise..."

"Would you mind sending a deputy over there?" Kim said.

Sheriff Jones nodded. "But you're not even sure they're here in Tennessee, isn't that right?"

Charlie shook his head. "I hate to admit it, but we're forced to make some assumptions... flying a little blind right now."

The sheriff nodded. "All right, I understand. Whatever you need. I can send one of my men to the airport, but it'll only leave two to knock on those doors. I can call in some more, if you think—"

"We'll take whatever we can get," Charlie said. "And we do really appreciate the help." He turned to Kim. "We should get heading down to Oak Ridge ourselves. If they're here, we're half a day behind."

Sheriff Jones looked at his watch. "I'll go get those deputies moving. And as soon as one of 'em has anything, I'll have them contact you directly."

Charlie pointed to the paper in the sheriff's hands. "Both our cell phones are on top."

Kim looked at Charlie. "You think we should go by the airport ourselves?"

Charlie shook his head, turned back to the sheriff. "The sooner you can get someone out there to Oliver Springs, the better. They get off the ground somehow, we're back to square one."

"Yes, sir," the sheriff said with a nod. He started for the building.

"Oh, and make sure your team's aware they're armed and dangerous. All three of them." Charlie turned and started back toward the Tahoe.

"Deputy," the sheriff said, "You don't have a vehicle description?"

Charlie shook his head. "Had him on camera, parked in a garage in Charlotte with a black Mercedes. But police found the car in the lot. They left it behind. So, no. We don't have a description yet."

"Too bad," the sheriff said. "Would be helpful we'd known what vehicle they were driving."

Charlie smirked and nodded, continued walking toward the Tahoe. "*No shit*," he said under his breath, pulling open the passenger-side door.

One of the deputies followed behind Kim and Charlie in the Tahoe, heading south on Route 61 before turning onto 9.

Kim had her eyes on the road and Charlie looked for the Briar Cliff subdivision where Jack Thornton had a cousin who lived there.

"There it is," Charlie said as soon as he saw the oversized McMansion-type homes built of full brick, with yards so small you could mow before the commercial breaks during the game were over.

Kim turned the wheel and pulled in the driveway of 4014 Hampstead Heath Drive. She stopped behind the black Range Rover with Tennessee plates parked in front of the third garage door on the right.

Charlie stepped out from the Tahoe and took a few steps down the driveway, the deputy walking toward him. "Go around back," Charlie said. "We'll respect the property, but keep our guard up, if you know what I mean?"

The deputy nodded and disappeared around the side of the house.

Kim knocked on the front door, and a little girl—about five or six years old— opened it just as Charlie walked up the steps.

Kim leaned down, her hands on her knees, and smiled at the girl. "Hey, sweetie. My name's Kim." She pointed with her thumb over her shoulder at Charlie, glancing back at him. "This is Charlie." She said to the little girl, "Is your mommy or daddy home?"

The little girl didn't say a word, her eyes down around Charlie's belt.

He saw she was looking at his Glock in the holster on his hip.

The girl shook her head. "Mommy's in the shower."

Kim stood up straight, looked in through the doorway over the little girl. "Would you mind telling Mommy there's someone at the door who would like to speak with her right away?"

The girl looked at Charlie. "Are you a policeman?"

Charlie had his eyes going through the open door into the house. He nodded. "Uh-huh." He was trying to see whatever was inside, on the other side of the doorway. He didn't like the feeling he had, wondered if someone was in there, sent the little girl to the door hoping they'd just go away. "Has your mommy had any visitors lately?"

The little girl opened her mouth and started to nod.

But a woman with long dark hair, wearing a tank top and shorts and a towel wrapped around her head, pulled the little girl back from the doorway. "Go on and clean up your room like I told you to, okay?" The woman looked at Charlie and Kim. "Can I help you?"

Charlie said, "You Clara Thornton?"

The woman paused, swallowed, and finally nodded her head, keeping her eyes on Charlie. "Is something wrong?"

"No, ma'am," he said. "I'm Deputy U.S. Marshal Charlie Harlow. This is Deputy U.S. Marshal Kim Riggins. We're looking for some people I believe you know. Friends of your husband's cousin. Any chance you know or've seen Jack's friend, Roger Flynn? Or maybe your husband has?"

"Roger?" she said, shaking her head. "We haven't see him in, God, I don't know... it's been a long time." She straightened out the towel on her head with both hands.

"So you do know who he is?" Charlie said.

Clara nodded. "Yes, but—"

"Would you mind if we came inside?" Kim said.

Clara seemed to hesitate. "Um, actually... I have to be somewhere shortly. If you want to ask me any questions, I'd be glad to answer right here."

"Ma'am, we won't take much of your time at all," Charlie said.

She stared back at him and slowly nodded, backing away from the door.

Charlie and Kim both stepped inside the house, the ceiling in the foyer a good twenty feet high with a crystal chandelier hanging over their heads. The place had a smell like new construction and fresh paint.

"You live here long?" Charlie said, looking around. He looked down the hallway and started toward the kitchen at the back of the house.

Clara made it in there ahead of him. "We just moved in a few weeks ago," she said.

Charlie looked out through the sliding glass door into the backyard. "Roger get a chance to check out the new place yet?" He gave the lady a smirk he couldn't hold back.

"No sir. Like I said, we haven't seen Roger in a long time."

"You recall when that might've been?" Kim said.

She shook her head. "No."

The little girl walked into the kitchen and had her eyes on Charlie again. She had a teddy bear in her arms and was sucking her thumb.

Her mom said, "Sweetie, why don't you go upstairs. Mommy will come up as soon as we're done."

Charlie had stepped around Clara and looked in the sink at five empty coffee cups. With his back to her, he said, "You have guests over this morning?"

She stepped next to Charlie and said, "Excuse me," practically nudging him out of the way. She took the cups from the sink and put them in the dishwasher. "A couple of neighbors stopped by this morning, to introduce themselves." She closed the dishwasher and wiped her hands with a dish towel folded next to the sink.

"Oh yeah?" he said. "Must be a very neighborly kind of neighborhood." He grinned and gave Kim a look, like he wasn't buying it one bit.

"I know what you're thinking," she said, shaking her head. "I assure you we haven't seen or heard from Roger. That's the truth. I wouldn't even let him in my home if he showed up." She swallowed and looked Charlie in the eye. "Did he really kill Jack?"

Charlie held his gaze. "We believe so."

She turned back to the sink and took whatever else was left in there—cups and a couple of spoons—and put them in the dishwasher. She turned back to Charlie and Kim, had tears in her eyes.

Charlie said, "If you don't mind..." He handed her his business card. "If you see or hear anything from or about Roger being back in town, would you please give us a call?"

Kim had stepped out of the kitchen, looking around the house ahead of Charlie.

The little girl came up and pulled on Charlie's shirt.

He turned to her as she handed him a piece of paper and ran off through the kitchen.

"Ellie May," the mother yelled. "What are you—" She stopped when Charlie held up what the little girl had handed him: A LYNX ticket for a one-way trip on the commuter rail in Charlotte.

Chapter 18

SHERIFF JONES AND FOUR deputies walked around inside and outside the home in the Briar Cliff subdivision looking for other clues.

Clara Flynn sat on the front brick steps with her little girl, Ellie May, just inside the house on the other side of the glass storm door.

Clara had confessed that Roger, Bella Ray, and Elizabeth Thornton forced Clara's husband—Jack's cousin, Billy—to take them somewhere in his car.

"He swore if I told you they were here, he'd kill Billy." She turned and looked through the open door at Ellie May, playing with her dolls on the hardwood floor. "He made me swear not to say a word if anyone came looking for him." She wiped her tears and her nose with the crumpled tissue she had in her hand.

"Holding back anything else at this point isn't going to help you or your husband," Charlie said. "Or... Ellie May."

Clara shook her head. "I'm *telling* you the truth. I don't know where they were going. Billy doesn't even have his cellphone… it's right inside. They wouldn't let him take it, so I wouldn't track him down, see where they were going."

Charlie turned from her when he saw Sheriff Jones come around from the back of the house. "Any word from your deputy over at Oliver Springs?"

The sheriff shook his head. "Quiet over there so far, from what he said."

Charlie turned back to Clara, his foot up on the bottom brick step, two steps down from where she sat. "Why didn't they just take your husband's car themselves? What'd they need Billy for?"

Clara looked down at Charlie, shaking her head with a shrug at the same time. She didn't seem to have an answer.

Charlie's phone buzzed in his pocket. He turned from the stairs and said, "Excuse me." He stood a few feet away in the driveway, looked at the screen and put the phone up to his ear. "Frank?"

"Just got off the phone with the Nashville office. They're sending a couple deputy marshals your way, assuming you could use a little more manpower."

"I don't know if it's necessarily manpower I need right now. But if they can help me get just one half step ahead of Flynn and the ladies, I'm all for it."

Frank paused on the other end of the line. "You know how much I hate to give you any credit, Charlie. But that gut of yours at least got you heading in the right direction. He can't be very far already, can he?"

Charlie glanced over at Clara. "Well, Roger and his girlfriends have the cousin behind the wheel, and the wife—Clara Thornton—appears to be telling the truth… she doesn't know where they went. Now, one thing I can't help wondering is if the cousin's actually in on whatever they're after."

"Has to be more than just a hostage situation, doesn't it?" Frank said.

"Yeah, well there's that." Charlie turned back to the house and saw little Ellie May looking out at him through the open doorway from inside the house.

Frank said, "Maybe we gotta treat it as a hostage situation for now. At least until we know otherwise."

"Still doesn't make sense why they didn't just take Billy Thornton's car. He must know something Jack might've shared with him."

"I still say, for now, we assume that man is a hostage. I don't want you to go after four of them, guns blazing… take down an innocent man. You got it?"

Charlie nodded into the phone. "Yeah, I got it."

"Just do what you have to do to get Roger Flynn, preferably alive, and his two lady friends."

"Three," Charlie said.

"As I just said, Charlie. Consider one of 'em a hostage." Frank hung up.

Charlie looked at the screen on his phone and tucked it back in his pocket. He walked back over to the stairs. Kim was on the top step, looking inside the house. "Where's Clara?" He stepped up onto the landing and saw Clara inside on the hardwood floor, playing with Ellie May. He leaned close to Kim and whispered into her ear. "Frank doesn't want to hear it, but I can't help thinking Billy Thornton's more than just an innocent bystander taken hostage."

Clara looked up at him through the open door.

Kim shrugged and the two stepped away from the door, down onto the grass. "What's it matter?"

"Well, it might matter when we're up against four of them. You think we're trying to help this guy, he pulls a weapon, starts firing..."

Kim looked Charlie in the eye and nodded. "But I understand where Frank's coming from."

Charlie walked up the steps and onto the landing. "Clara?" He smiled at Ellie May when she and her mother looked up.

Clara got up off the floor and stepped outside.

Charlie kept his voice low so Ellie May couldn't hear. "I just want you to understand, you're putting your little girl in real danger if your husband's involved with a man like Roger Flynn. Anything else you can tell me..."

"I told you everything I know."

"But what was his involvement with Jack? He must've known—"

"I don't know. They kept in touch, maybe even more so after Jack got in trouble."

"And Roger just showed up here? Out of the blue?" He looked through the doorway. "But you took the time to make him coffee, didn't you?"

She shook her head. "There was nothing we could do. We had no idea he'd show up here. He forced Billy to—"

"Forced him?" Charlie said. "You mean, at gunpoint?"

Clara nodded. A tear came down her cheek. "Billy tried to tell him to just take one of the cars. He didn't want to go with him, tried to give him options. That's when Roger pulled the gun, put it right in Billy's back."

Charlie gave Kim a quick glance, then turned his eyes back to Clara. "You mind we talk to Ellie May in private?"

Clara shook her head. "No. Please. She's already upset enough, she—"

"She doesn't look too upset," he said, looking down at her playing with the dolls on the floor. "In fact, she doesn't look like a kid whose Daddy got dragged out the door with a gun in his back."

Clara folded her arms across her chest, her eyes down on the bricks below. She stayed quiet for a couple of moments, finally raising her eyes to Charlie and Kim. She wiped a tear from her eye with the back of her hand. "He was driving them to the airport. They had a plane waiting."

"Oliver Springs?" Kim said.

Clara shook her head. "Billy has a friend in Jamestown—owns a small airport. Mostly just private planes fly in and out of there." She swallowed and said, "I'm sorry. I just... my little girl."

"Anything else you want to tell us?" Charlie said, taking his phone from his pocket to call Frank.

"No, I swear. I don't know anything else."

Charlie was about to dial the phone. "You keep saying you don't know nothing else, but then you keep coming up with more." He took a breath, shaking his head. "I'd hate to have to ask one of these deputies to take you in, your little girl'd have to be taken into custody... end up in a home she's never been for the night."

Clara shook her head. "No, please. I swear, I've told you everything I know." The tears were flowing now, coming down both sides of Clara's cheeks.

"Just so I'm clear," Charlie said, "Are you now telling me your husband willingly drove Roger and the two ladies to that airport?"

She looked back toward the doorway. "Billy didn't have a choice. But Roger didn't have to hold a gun on him, like I'd said."

Chapter 19

JAMESTOWN WAS OVER AN hour away from Oak Ridge, Tennessee, and Charlie knew they were too far behind Roger and the two women. Frank had already contacted the chief of police in Jamestown and filled him in. Checkpoints and roadblocks were set along Routes 127, 329, and Tennessee 52... the only major roads leading to and from the Jamestown Municipal Airport. The locals had checked every car that had driven through the airport's entrance.

Charlie was behind the wheel of Kim's Tahoe, made the one-hour-twenty-minute trip in fifty-seven minutes with Kim buckled in the passenger seat. But there hadn't been any sightings and nothing more than a couple of single engines on the runway since morning, according to the Jamestown officer and the deputy marshal who'd made it over from the Nashville office to help.

Charlie leaned against the Tahoe with one foot crossed over the other. He looked up into the blue sky and shook his head. "Either Clara lied to us or they told her something everyone but Clara knew wasn't true." He gave Kim a nod. "Might as well go look around the hangars, maybe see a plane in there someone was getting prepared but couldn't get in the air."

Kim followed him through the terminal and outside through the back by the hangar.

Charlie looked out toward the runway, saw the Cessna he'd been told was there all morning and hadn't moved.

An older gentleman with a limp walked toward them, dressed in a dark khaki-colored one-piece: uniform-like but without visible patches or some sort of name or company stitched over the chest. He looked at Charlie with a nod. "I know you're supposed to be looking for someone, but I can't keep this place shut down all day. It's costing money. And the longer my customers have to wait to take off..."

"I understand," Charlie said. "We'll be out of your hair as soon as we can." He looked out toward another small plane parked around the side of the building. "Who's that?"

"The Piper? What about it?"

"It in use?"

The man shook his head. "No, sir. Won't be in operation for maybe another day or two."

Charlie looked in the other direction toward one of the planes he'd been told was there all morning, parked a good distance down the far end of the runway almost near the chain-link fence. But it was parked facing the terminal. "What's that one doing all the way out there?"

"The Cessna?" The man shrugged. "Been parked there all day."

"Anybody inside?"

The man shook his head. "I don't believe so."

Charlie looked back at the terminal, saw another man dressed in khakis and a blue short-sleeve golf shirt. The man was watching Charlie from the other side of a glass door but stepped away and disappeared. Charlie turned back and looked toward the Cessna. "How many passengers that plane carry?"

"Three, plus the pilot."

Charlie pulled out his phone and pulled up a photo of Roger Stone. "I assume you've already been asked this question, but any chance you recognize this man?"

The man shook his head. "No, sir. Never seen him before in my life."

"You sure?" Charlie looked the man in the eye.

"Yeah, I'm sure. Never seem 'im."

Charlie ran his finger over the phone's screen and turned it to the man once again. He showed him the photo of Liz and Bella Ray. "What about these two? You recognize either one of 'em?"

The man shook his head. "Sure are pretty though."

One of the Jamestown police officers, a heavy-looking man, ran toward Charlie from the terminal. "Charlie, hey…" He stopped, his hands on his hips, gasping for air and trying to catch his breath. "The man you were looking for—one of them—was just pulled over driving his Land Cruiser over on Route 52. He was heading south."

"Billy Thornton?" Charlie said.

The officer nodded. "Yes sir, that's him. He's in custody back at the station."

Charlie hurried toward the terminal, far ahead of the officer.

The officer had a job to keep up with Charlie's long steps. "Said he was doing about eighty-four when he was pulled over."

"Nobody else in the car?" Charlie said, stopping to hold the door for the officer.

"No, just the one man."

Charlie stood out front of the terminal and looked around. "Shit," he said. He turned to Kim, right behind him. "Might as well tell everyone we're sorry we wasted their time." He started toward the Tahoe, was sure they'd missed them once again. But he stopped when he heard the sound of a plane's engine starting. He ran by Kim and back through the terminal building, came out the door by the hangar.

The Cessna parked on the far end of the runway was taxiing toward him and picking up speed.

Kim and two officers ran out from the terminal door behind him.

Charlie turned to them. "Where are those two men who were out here?" He looked around but didn't see a soul anywhere. He yelled to nobody in particular, "*Who in the hell's flying that plane?*" He started walking down the runway toward it. "Who the hell gave them the okay to take off?"

He started to run.

The plane accelerated, coming straight at him running toward it, like a game of chicken.

"Charlie!" Kim yelled, running after him. "What the hell are you doing?"

Charlie pulled out his Glock as he ran, held it in one hand and pulled out his badge with the other. He ran as fast as he could toward it. "Stop that plane!" he yelled, waving the badge as if the pilot or anyone inside could hear him. "Stop!"

The plane continued toward him, picking up speed until it lifted off the ground so close to Charlie's head, he ducked and fell to the pavement. The plane was airborne.

Charlie looked up from a crouched position and saw the Cessna making a turn with a slight tilt, going back the other way and circling around over the building. He held up the Glock, tempted to pull the trigger and take the thing right out of the sky.

"Charlie, no!" Kim yelled, running toward him with her Glock in her hand. She helped him off the ground. "Charlie, we can't."

He got to his feet and tucked the Glock into his holster.

But the plane had turned around, coming back at them and flying low enough he could see the pilot and her short, buzzed hair and aviator glasses over her eyes. The plane turned, almost daring him to shoot, and came back around so Charlie could see someone looking out at him through the small round window on the side.

Bella Ray Sparrow was looking down at him, a big smile on her face. She waved and blew him a kiss as the plane climbed higher into the sky and disappeared into the clouds.

Chapter 20

BILLY THORNTON HADN'T BEEN handcuffed or held against his wishes, just stood waiting with the officers off Route 52 where he'd been pulled over in his Land Cruiser, when Charlie and Kim pulled up behind them.

Charlie stepped down from the Tahoe and slammed the passenger door, charged past the officers and toward Billy without a word. He grabbed Billy by the shirt with both hands. He threw him against one of the two Jamestown Police vehicles and pinned his back against the Range Rover's hood, the man's feet dangling off the ground over the bumper.

The officers didn't seem to want to get in his way, but Kim pulled at Charlie's shirt and grabbed him from behind, trying to pull him off Billy.

But Charlie wasn't about to let go. "*Where'd they go?*" he yelled, his teeth clenched tight together, spit coming from his mouth like a rabid dog.

Billy Thornton didn't look like what Charlie'd expected for someone driving a Range Rover. The guy looked like your average truck-driving redneck the way he was dressed, but somehow'd come into money. Charlie had an idea about that.

With Charlie holding Billy by the shirt, barking at him, the fear could be seen in Billy's eyes.

The officers stood still, let Charlie do whatever he had to, to get the man to talk.

"I-I already told them," Billy said, stammering. "I-I don't know where they went. I swear. I dropped Roger and the girls at the airport. That was all he asked me to do."

Charlie pulled Billy off the hood and let him stand on his own two feet but held onto his shirt with one hand. "Then how the hell'd they get out to that runway without being seen?"

"They climbed the fence on the other side. It was early, before there was anyone inside." He shrugged. "They might've known someone working there, but they didn't tell me."

"And you're going to look me in the eye and try to tell me you have no idea where they've gone?"

Billy shook his head. "Roger wouldn't say." He nodded at the officers. "I told them already... Roger says I got a big mouth."

Kim stepped between Charlie and Billy. "I suggest you start talking." She looked Billy in the eye. "Unless you want to end up behind bars where you'll have plenty of time to think all by yourself. Harboring a criminal is at least five years."

Charlie said, "And we can always push for more than that," just to see if they could get the guy talking. "Ten or twenty... your little girl'll be ready for college... maybe off and married when you get out."

Billy shook his head. "I'm telling you the truth. I don't know anything. I had no choice."

"Is that so?" Charlie said, turning away and glancing at the officers watching him. He turned back to Billy. "What's he paying you?"

Billy took a moment before he answered. "He's not paying me nothing."

Charlie walked over to the Range Rover and looked inside, then looked back at the officers. "Find anything in here?"

One of the officers walked toward Charlie, shaking his head. "Not a thing."

Charlie stepped back toward Billy, leaning on the front fender of the officer's cruiser. "There something you knew about something... is that why Roger came to you?"

Billy stared at Charlie. "He asked me about money Jack must've hidden somewhere. I told him I didn't know nothing about it. It's not like Jack and I were that close the last couple of years."

"So, then what? You didn't know anything about what he was looking for, offered them a ride?"

Billy shook his head. "I just wanted to get them out of the house. My little girl..." He shook his head and looked out toward the cars buzzing along the highway, drivers tapping their brakes when they were close enough to see the police vehicles.

"So, would you explain to me," Charlie said, "why you didn't just let him take the car? Instead of you driving him, getting yourself mixed up with all this?"

Billy shrugged. "He woulda left it at the airport... I gotta work, you know."

Charlie was on the phone with Frank on the ride back to Asheville, Kim back behind the wheel. Charlie had to hear it for letting Roger and the two ladies take off on a plane everyone knew was right there on the runway, not even a hundred yards from where Charlie stood.

Charlie said, "I'm not going to place blame on the Jamestown Police Department, but the fact is I was told they looked in the plane and nobody was inside it."

Frank said, "Well, somehow they got in there."

Charlie glanced at Kim then turned, looked out the window at the mountains. "Jack's cousin Billy said they hopped the fence. I imagine they waited for the right time... had someone park the plane way down the other end of the runway."

"So then someone from that airport was involved?" Frank said. "Because, I don't know if you've ever been inside a Cessna, but there ain't no way they were hiding in there the whole time."

"There was a couple gentlemen there," Charlie said, "and one disappeared before I could ask him any questions. Dressed like he worked there." He scratched the back of his neck. "But now I'm not sure."

"Well, truth is," Frank said, "it doesn't matter where they were or how they got in there when everyone was supposedly looking for them. Fact is, they're gone now." He paused. "Again." Frank hung up the phone.

Charlie stared at the screen then turned, had his eyes out the passenger window. After a couple moments he turned to Kim. "He's not too happy."

Kim kept her eyes on the road. "Can you blame him?"

"Of course not. I... I just wish we'd looked a little more, instead of trusting those officers. Small town like that, I can't imagine they're used to doing much of anything outside running speed traps and handing out parking tickets."

Kim gave him a quick glance. "You're going to blame the Jamestown Police Department? We're as much to blame as anyone."

Charlie didn't respond, although he knew she was right. "I just don't understand... an old man like Roger Flynn, you'd think it'd be easy."

"Old men are wise," Kim said. "Like Whitey Bulger. How many years it take to finally track him down?"

Charlie shook his head, turned his gaze outside the window to his right. "I'm not going to be around another twenty years trying to find Roger Flynn. There comes a point..."

The two drove quiet for a good part of the ride, Charlie putting his head back with his hat over his eyes trying to catch a nap. But he couldn't get comfortable and wasn't as tired as he thought. He lifted his head. "You mind if I call Jennie?"

Kim said, "No, I don't mind. But Jennie might." She glanced at Charlie and grinned, then turned her eyes back to the road.

"What's that supposed to mean?" he said, staring back at Kim.

"I was kidding, I guess."

"You guess?"

She glanced at him one more time. "Maybe you give her some space, she won't act the way she does toward you."

"Oh, I don't think it would make much of a difference." He smiled and straightened his hat on his head. "Besides... can't I still be worried about her, even if we're not together?"

"I know you always worry about her," Kim said, nodding. "But Rivers is at the house, isn't he? And nobody even knows if Hunter King's still in the area. Who knows if he's even alive?"

"We're supposed to believe he was at that mobile park with his brother," Charlie said. "According to three separate witnesses. Down from six."

Kim kept her eyes on the road. "You sound like you don't believe it."

"Do I?" Charlie slouched back in the passenger seat, put his boot up on the dash and turned to his right, looking out the window. "If it wasn't Hunter there with his brother, it was someone else, made that gun disappear."

"You think that's possible?" Kim had her eyes on Charlie for a moment. "Or if Gunner was the one who pulled that trigger... who knows if someone saw the gun on the ground next to him, took off with it."

"I'm not sure I believe some random passerby just picked it up. I'm saying everyone's out there looking for Hunter, but nobody's seen him in months. But anything's possible. But I still can't help worrying about Jennie." He turned and gazed out at the mountains along Route 40.

After another five or so miles of quiet between the two, the only sound coming from a Johnny Cash CD, Charlie straightened out in his seat. "So how'd we go from me wanting to call Jennie... to a random suspect picking up the gun used to shoot Deputy Moore? This something you'd already been tossing around in your mind, or—"

"Frank agreed to let Kyle keep an eye on Jennie because he knew you were concerned. But I got the feeling he wasn't convinced he believed she was in real danger." She turned to Charlie with a grin. "If she was, you think he'd trust Kyle?"

Charlie was somewhat confused, cocked his head back a bit, looking at Kim. "You telling me Frank thinks I used this as an excuse to keep an eye on Jennie? Use our limited resources just to—"

"I think you feel better having someone down there watching her just in case. I'd hate to be the one who'd deny her protection and something happened. I'm sure Frank's thinking the same thing."

"But he's doing it just to *appease* me?"

Kim shook her head. "I think I'm making some assumptions, Charlie. Don't go blaming Frank for something." She paused. "Either way, Frank's not going to take the chance of having your ex-wife in danger, I can promise you that."

Charlie looked straight ahead, toward the road. "She's not officially my ex, you know."

Chapter 21

It was late when Charlie drove down to Hendersonville in Lindsey's Ford Taurus, tired from the long day that didn't want to end. He pulled in the driveway of what was still legally his house, the curtains closed on the picture window, light slipping through the slits into the dark outside.

He stood with the car's door open and looked over his shoulder at Deputy Marshal Rivers still parked out in the road.

Kyle had already stepped outside his car, walking toward Charlie. "I wasn't sure who you were," he said. "Where'd you get that car?"

Charlie looked back at the Taurus. "Friend of mine's." He walked toward Kyle and looked back at the house, assumed Jennie was inside alone since he didn't see any other car. He said to Kyle, "Pretty quiet?"

Kyle nodded. "She hasn't been shot, if that's what you mean?"

Charlie made a face, wanted to slap the kid upside the head. "What the hell's wrong with you, saying something like that?" He shook his head and started back up the driveway.

"What'd I say?" Kyle said, standing at the end of the driveway. "Charlie?"

Charlie didn't look back or answer Kyle, stepped up the front steps and knocked on the door. He leaned back to watch the curtain move to the side, Jennie looking out like she couldn't see anyone.

The locks on the door clicked and Jennie opened it. "Charlie?" she said. "What are you doing here?" She backed away from the doorway to let him in. "I told you I'd appreciate it you'd call before coming down here, showing up out of the blue like this."

Charlie shrugged, nodding. "I know." He looked her up and down, pretty as always. He looked in toward the kitchen.

"Everything all right with you?" Jennie said. "You look tired."

"I *am* tired," he said, scratching his cheek as he looked around like he thought he'd find something. Or some*one*. He turned back to her.

On the drive down from Asheville he'd thought about what he could've done different... if he could've fixed himself before their marriage fell apart. Maybe if he'd let go of the rush he got being a deputy U.S. Marshal... get a regular job, maybe work local law enforcement, stop home for lunch with Jennie once or twice a week.

He gazed into her eyes and grinned, pushing his hair off his forehead. He turned and stepped to the window, pushed the curtain aside and looked out at Kyle Rivers back in the driver's seat of the car. He wondered if the kid was even awake. "I'm not sure you need Kyle out there any longer." He turned from the window. "Truth is, you may not be in any kind of real danger at this point."

Jennie looked him in the eye with a slight squint, staring back at him like she could see deep into his soul and trying to read what was going through his mind. "Good," she said. "I can have my life back, then?" She kept her gaze on Charlie. "Honestly, Charlie, I wasn't even a bit scared something was going to happen. I don't know why. I guess I couldn't help but think nobody'd go after a man's ex-wife. In a lot of cases, they'd be doing the man a favor."

Charlie shook his head. "You're not technically my ex-wife, Jennie. But if you were, I certainly wouldn't consider something happening to you being a favor of any sort. But I know what you mean. I have a feeling Frank and Kim were thinking the same thing."

She stood quiet and folded her arms across her chest. "Now that you bring it up... what do I have to do to get you to sign those divorce papers, Charlie? We can't stay like this, in limbo. Not together anymore but legally tied together like we are because you can't bring yourself to sign your name, make it official."

Charlie rolled his eyes. "We're talking about your safety and well-being, and you're worried about—"

"Jesus, Charlie. I'm fine. You hardly see a damn car go down this road after sunset." She stepped to the window and pulled the curtain back. "He leaving tonight? Or are we going to have to stretch this out any longer?"

"Like our divorce?" Charlie said, smiling... a joke made at his own expense.

He watched her turn from the window and heard what he knew was a gunshot, saw a flash of light in the darkness across the street outside. The cuckoo clock that'd belonged to Jennie's grandmother fell from the wall and crashed to the floor, glass from the picture window shattered.

"Get down!" Charlie yelled as he tackled Jennie, took her down to the floor but away from the window's broken glass along the edge of the rug on the hardwoods. He covered over her and pulled out his gun.

More shots were fired, coming from somewhere outside. Charlie heard Kyle yell something but wasn't sure what it was and wasn't sure Kyle was all right. He had to get Jennie out of harm's way. They both stayed low under the window sill, Charlie holding Jennie's hand, pulling her toward the middle of the house and into the hallway toward the bedrooms. "You okay?" he said and she nodded. "Stay low. And don't move."

Another shot was fired.

Charlie had his Glock out and up in front of him, hunched over low as he stepped over the glass and toward the door. More shots were fired, one after the other, coming through the windows and through the side of the house. He remained still, listening after he'd counted sixteen rounds.

He looked toward the kitchen, tempted to go out the back door, but figured whoever'd fired those shots could be long gone if he didn't get out there. He reached for the doorknob and pulled open the front door. He was down in a crouched position behind the wall, stuck his head out and yelled for Kyle to stay down, only assuming the kid was all right.

Charlie pointed his Glock, his finger on the trigger, but another shot was fired, this time taking out the lamp outside over the door. He was sure he saw a flash where the shot fired from and took a shot himself in that direction.

He waited, listening. He stepped outside and jumped down the steps, kept low as he ran over the grass across the yard. He called for Kyle, thinking a shot into the dark wasn't the smartest thing he'd ever done.

"He's over here!" Kyle yelled.

Charlie ran, saw Kyle on the other side of the street with his gun drawn, pointing the muzzle toward the ground, but Charlie couldn't see enough to know what or who he was pointing at.

The light from the street lamp reflected off blood in the street as Charlie crossed and stood next to Kyle.

A man Charlie didn't recognize was on his back, looking up at the gun just inches from his face. He shook his head, his hands back but on the ground.

Kyle looked at Charlie and nodded with the excitement of a kid catching his first fish. "You got him!" he said. "You got him, Charlie."

Charlie crouched down and grabbed the man by the arm and dragged him to Kyle's car. He threw the man facedown on the hood and slapped the cuffs on his wrists. "This isn't Hunter King," he said. "Hunter King's ghost-white and a foot taller'n this guy." Charlie looked in Kyle's car and thought a moment. "Were you in your car this whole time?"

Kyle shook his head. "I was taking a leak, heard the first shot and, well, I couldn't see where they were coming from at first... so stayed down, went after him but you'd already fired a shot."

Charlie held his gaze on Kyle, holding the man pinned against the hood. "You were taking a leak?" He didn't wait for Kyle's answer, lifted the man from the hood and turned him around. He saw how much blood was soaked through the man's shirt. "We'd better get the paramedics out here."

"I already called," Kyle said.

Charlie dragged the man to the side of the car and grabbed him by the top of his shirt. "What's your name?"

The man stared without much expression. He didn't answer.

Charlie knew the man was of Latin descent, maybe didn't speak English. "Cómo te llamas?" Charlie said.

No answer.

Charlie reached around and into the man's back pocket, pulled out a wallet and flipped through what was inside, tossing things to the ground until he found an ID. "Alejandro Gomez, from Tennessee." He looked at Kyle. "You see a vehicle?"

Kyle shook his head.

Charlie took his hands from the man's shirt and felt the warm, wet blood on them. He looked around into the darkness. "Could be someone else out there," he said, then turned to the man. "Alejandro, who'd you come here with? Who sent you?"

Alejandro seemed to be aware, at least somewhat, but still hadn't said a word.

"You sure he's all right?" Kyle said, standing behind Charlie now.

Charlie looked closer into the man's eyes. Charlie said, "Alejandro? Me escuchas?"

"What'd you say?" Kyle said.

"I asked him if he could hear me."

Sirens screamed in the distance, growing louder, the blue and red lights coming through the trees.

Charlie eased Alejandro to the ground, leaned him up against the car. "I gotta go check on Jennie." He nodded to Kyle. "Keep an eye on him." He started for the house.

Kyle said, "Is he alive?"

"What do you mean *is he alive*?" Charlie stopped and turned to Kyle, thought for a moment then walked back across the road. He crouched down in front of Alejandro and looked into his eyes, still open but distant. Charlie reached under the man's chin, felt for a pulse and held it there for a moment. He took his hand away, wiped it on his pants and stood up, shaking his head. "Shit," he said. "He's dead."

Chapter 22

Frank closed the door behind Charlie and sat back down at his desk. He nodded toward the chairs across from him. "Have a seat."

Charlie sat down and leaned forward on the chair, his elbows on his knees, hands clasped together.

Frank pulled his glasses from his face and wiped his hand over his eyes. "I hope you realize what you're going to be up against," Frank said. "Now, I'm not saying it wasn't warranted, man opens fire on your ex-wife's—"

"Jennie's not my ex yet," he said.

Frank rolled his eyes. "Charlie, you're being investigated by the US Attorney General's Office for shooting a man we still can't prove was the one pulled the trigger on a weapon we've yet to find. Now we've got another one with a bullet inside him's got your name on it... and you weren't even on the clock."

Charlie leaned back in the chair. "Come on, Frank. This one's pretty cut-and-dried. I mean, anyone expect me to hold my fire, got bullets flying every which way at my and Jennie's heads?"

Frank sighed. "No, of course not." He picked up a piece of paper from a folder, looked it over and placed it back down on the desk. "I'm just frustrated, that's all. You know how this all works as much as anybody. And the last thing I need right now is to be a man down for a few months, the way they'll drag this out... if you're not suspended, you'll be on the desk for ten, twelve months now. Department of Justice will do that, you know, they feel they need to."

Charlie smirked. "Maybe you can have Kyle out there to replace me."

Frank sighed and shook his head. "Christ, I'm real sorry about that, Charlie. I really didn't think we had anything to worry about."

"Well, you were right about one thing. It wasn't Hunter King. And besides, Kyle hadn't gone to take a leak he would've been sitting there in the driver's seat... a dead duck."

"I guess that's one way of looking at it," Frank said, shaking his head. "What is it with these young guys? That's twice now—including Gilson at the hotel—got some impeccable timing for knowing when to hit the head."

Charlie huffed out a slight laugh.

Frank stood up from his desk. "I'm just glad everyone's all right. I mean, other than Mr. Gomez." He put his hand on Charlie's shoulder as he walked toward the door. He stopped. "Oh, and there's a Chevy Suburban downstairs, came off the repo lot. Since I assume Lindsey'd like the Taurus back..."

Charlie had finished his second bourbon by the time Lindsey had stopped to talk to him, the Coyote Grille busier than it had been since the night before his car was blown to pieces.

Lindsey leaned on the bar in front of him, her hands out wide from her shoulders.

"Those boys never showed up again?" Charlie said, holding his glass just under his chin.

Lindsey shook her head. "I'm kind of surprised you hadn't tracked them down yourself by now, teach them a lesson even if they weren't the ones who blew up your car."

"It's not the job of the U.S. Marshal Service to investigate or even go after criminals merely suspected of committing a crime. We're not involved until we have a warrant in our hands."

Lindsey grinned. "I know. You've told me that before. I just meant—"

"I don't think anyone's interested in trying to track down two idiots unless there's reason to believe they're the ones who blew up my car. But, nah, the bomb wasn't something someone could throw together after a bar fight."

Lindsey straightened up off the bar, gave Charlie a look. "I just wish you'd come in a little sooner, make sure I was all right. I didn't even have a car..."

Charlie had the glass up near his lips but put it back down on the bar. "I'm sorry. You're right. I should've at least called. It's just..." He raised his glass and took a sip. "Someone let off a round of bullets, nearly killed me and my, uh... nearly killed Jennie. Thought they were after her, but turns out someone had followed me down there, likely having something to do with the man we've been chasing from here to Tennessee.

She smiled back at him. "I'm just giving you shit, Charlie. I know you're a lawman, got a life of your own. No need to stop and worry about the bartender you come see when you're lonely."

Charlie dropped his shoulders. "Come on, Lindsey. That's not all it is." He finished what was in his glass, slid it across the bar. "Maybe I can make it up to you somehow?"

Lindsey rolled her eyes and gave him a crooked grin, took his empty glass and dropped in a couple of ice cubes... poured him a double.

The light from outside poured into the bar and Charlie turned to the door to see who'd just walked in.

Kim squeezed in between Charlie and the stool next to him, turned to face him. "You don't answer your phone?"

Charlie swallowed hard, shaking his head. "Huh?" He reached in his pocket and looked at the screen, saw Kim had called him six times. All within the past half hour. "Sorry," he said. "Had the ringer turned down when—"

"We have communication from Alejandro Gomez's phone, tracked at least a half dozen calls to and from a hotel down in Charleston, South Carolina."

"Charleston?" Charlie said. "Any ideas? Maybe Flynn?"

Kim nodded. "A Cessna was spotted, touched down in a regional airport down that way, just outside Charleston. Town called Mount Pleasant."

Charlie nodded. "I know where that is. Nice beach down there, Sullivan's Island. But what do you mean, *touched down*? I assume they landed there?"

Kim shrugged. "Didn't communicate with the tower. Almost crashed with another plane taking off. They landed off the strip and three people got off and disappeared. Plane took off a couple of minutes later."

Charlie tossed back what was left in the glass and wiped his mouth with the back of his hand. "You driving? I gotta leave the Ford here."

She stared back at Charlie, shaking her head. "Frank put in a request for the district office down there in South Carolina to handle it."

"You kidding me?" He shook his head and started for the door. "No way. Roger Flynn is mine." He tapped the screen of his phone, about to call Frank.

Kim reached for Charlie's phone and took it from his hand, ended the call before it went through. "You didn't let me finish," she said. "He *didn't* want us to go. But I got him to agree, told him I'd pick you up and we'd drive straight down. Deputies are on standby. We asked them not to make any moves until we get there."

"I'll drive... if you don't mind we swing by the office? Frank got me a big Suburban before it hit the auction. Might need the space in back, we nail all three of them." He was at the door but stopped and said to Kim, "I'll meet you outside. Give me a minute."

Kim walked out and Charlie turned to the bar, Lindsey with her back to him wiping down bottles.

Charlie cleared his throat and said, "You ignoring me on purpose?"

She looked over her shoulder at him. "I thought you were trying to sneak out without paying your tab."

He shook his head, kept his eyes on hers and pulled a couple of bills from his pocket. "Keep the change," he said. "I gotta head down to Charleston."

"I like Charleston," she said.

"Yeah, well too bad it's not for pleasure. If it was, maybe I'd take you with me." He gave her a nod. "This is why I have an ex, er, soon to be ex-wife. Not easy being involved with someone who chases after moving targets for a living."

She turned, holding a bottle in her hand, smiled back at him and brushed a strand of hair from her face. She looked down the bar, reached into the beer cooler and came up with two bottles of beer. She carried them over for two of her customers and set them down.

Charlie had his eyes on her, smiled when she turned back and stepped toward him.

"You know where to find me when you get back," she said, wiping down the space with a towel in front of him where he'd sat. She held her gaze on him for a moment, then turned, walked through the swinging door behind her and disappeared.

Charlie stood still for a moment, watching the door like he thought maybe she'd come back through. He turned for the main door to leave and looked back toward the bar one more time before he stepped outside.

Chapter 23

Rain came down hard for most of the drive down to Charleston, the wipers on the Suburban running back and forth, not doing much of a job keeping the windshield clear. Charlie looked over at Kim, her head turned from him looking out the passenger window.

Charlie said, "Wish I knew what this car smelled like before I took the keys." He took a good sniff. "Marijuana's all caught up in the air conditioning. Gonna have to have it cleaned out when we get back."

They went over the Ben Sawyer Bridge and crossed onto Sullivan's Island.

Kim said, "Turn here."

Charlie turned the wheel, went right onto Ben Sawyer Boulevard, then left onto Jasper to stay on 703. "What's the gentleman's name again?"

Kim turned to Charlie. "Jason Day. Elizabeth Thornton's former business associate, going back about five years ago." She turned her head and faced the passenger window, looking out toward the water and parked boats behind the buildings. "Owns both a boat *and* a private jet."

"And you said, what, he's got a ten-thousand-square-foot home? Right on the water?"

"Around that size, yes," Kim said.

Charlie stopped on Jasper, looked toward the modern square house, appearing to be mostly made of windows. He looked up at the third floor, thought he could see someone inside but it was hard to tell. "That it?"

"Looks like it," she said. "A lot of house for one man."

"No wife or kids or anything?" Charlie said.

Kim shook her head, her eyes up on the house.

The ocean was behind it, and in the front, on the other side of the enclosed fence with a gate and guardhouse was a fountain—not one of those little ones you buy at the home improvement store—built like something you'd see in a public park or town center. It wasn't exactly dark outside, but the clouds were heavy enough you could see the lights shine through the jets of water shooting thirty feet into the air.

"I don't see a guard at the gate. Any idea how we're getting inside?" Charlie said.

Kim shrugged. "I thought we'd just pull up and ask." She grinned, and Charlie wasn't sure if she was kidding or not.

He turned the wheel and pulled the Suburban into the driveway, felt like he was turning a bus. He stopped with the front bumper just inches from the gate, the rear end still stuck out in the road. The rain came down across the headlights but wasn't as heavy as it was for most of the ride down. He put down the window, reached his arm out into the rain and pressed the call button on the keypad. He glanced at Kim. "I don't know about this," he said. "I have a hard time believing a man Elizabeth Thornton worked with five years ago would help them hide on Sullivan's Island."

"The business relationship was five years ago, but investigations said their personal relationship continued beyond that. I don't know what kind of personal relationship... or what Jack thought of him."

Charlie nodded, accepting their small lead as better than nothing. He reached his arm out one more time and again pressed the button on the keypad. "Maybe nobody's home?" he said, looking through the gate toward the house.

Both Charlie and Kim jumped and reached for their guns when a man showed up on the other side of the gate in a yellow raincoat, the hood up over his head. He stared back out at them.

Charlie stuck his head out the driver's-side window. "We're looking for Mr. Jason Day. Any chance he's home?"

The man paused a moment, then shook his head. "He ain't here. You just missed him."

"Any idea where he went?" Charlie said.

The man stared back at Charlie. "He doesn't tell me where he's going. I'm just here tending to the gardens." He looked behind him, toward the house. "Good chance you'll find him over at the Shem Creek Boat Landing."

The rain had stopped; the sun was trying to break through the clouds. The man removed his hood and looked up at the sky.

Charlie stepped out from the Suburban and walked up to the gate, stood eye to eye with the man in the yellow raincoat. "Was Mr. Day alone?"

The man shrugged. "Not my place to tell you that," he said. "Like I said, I'm just here to—"

"Any chance one of 'em an older gentleman? White hair... two good-looking women with him?"

The man looked toward the Suburban and took a moment, then finally nodded. "Sounds about right." He turned from the gate and walked away without another word.

Charlie yelled, "Thank you, sir," and jumped back in the driver's side. He shifted into reverse and backed onto the wet road, spun the Suburban around and the wheels slipped, started back in the direction they were already heading. "Shem Creek Boat Landing," he said.

Kim punched it into the GPS.

They drove back over the bridge, toward the Shem Creek area.

"What kind of car's he drive?" Charlie said, putting a little more pressure with his foot on the pedal, speeding at a little over seventy before he slowed down to turn onto Coleman, then Simmons as Kim told him.

"He has ten cars, but the one he drives most is a Mercedes GLE-450. It's a white SUV," Kim said.

Charlie drove slow, kept his eyes out for the white Mercedes. He turned the wheel and pulled into the parking lot when he saw *Shem Creek Landing* carved and painted on the wooden sign. He drove between the rows of parked cars and turned the corner, pulled the Suburban up to the curb at the front entrance to the building.

He turned on the hazards and stepped out with Kim behind him. They both walked up to the door with OFFICE on a sign over the window, went inside and up to the only man in the place, seated behind a desk. "Excuse me, sir? I'm wondering if you can tell me where I might find a Mr. Jason Day?"

The man had his eyes down on his computer screen but looked up, shaking his head. "Haven't seen him today," he said. "But that doesn't mean he's not here. Might be out on the dock somewhere by his boat." The man's eyes went to the badge Charlie was holding. "You with the sheriff's office?"

Charlie shook his head and looked around the office and out through the windows on the back wall toward the docked boats. "Deputy U.S. Marshal."

"You serious?"

"Why wouldn't I be serious?"

The man shrugged. "I didn't know that was still a thing." He grinned. "Not since the Wild West."

Charlie said, "What slip is his boat at?"

"Jason? Dock G, slip thirteen."

"Lucky thirteen, huh?" Charlie pointed with his thumb toward the door. "I get out there going this way?"

The man seemed hesitant to answer. "Is there a problem I can help you with?"

Charlie didn't answer, walked out the front door with Kim right behind him. They walked past the Suburban in front of the marina's office, turned down a stone walkway and ducked under a thick rope. Charlie saw a sign for Dock G and counted the slips on the left side of the dock without walking down it: five, seven, nine, eleven… thirteen. He walked the dock and stopped, saw the number thirteen nailed to the piling.

Jason Day had a fishing boat, similar to one Charlie had recently taken from a couple up on Oak Island a few months back, after they had been charged with murdering the woman's father.

Charlie grabbed the aluminum rail and threw one leg over to step up onto the boat. He flipped the latch on the other side and helped Kim up behind him. He walked across the deck and took the ladder down below to the cabin. There were three beds—one full size, the others built-in singles—a TV on the wall, a good-sized wet bar, and four leather chairs around a table. He didn't see much that would tell him anything, turned and went back up the ladder.

He walked toward the helm, looked out at the water and all the boats docked and anchored in Shem Creek. He scanned the boats parked along the edge of the water and called for Kim.

He had his eyes on a restaurant on the edge of the creek, about seventy-five yards away. From what he could see, most of the outdoor tables were full. He opened a storage compartment at the helm and found a pair of binoculars, lifted them to his eyes and looked down toward the restaurant. He adjusted the focus as he scanned left to right. "Kim!" he yelled, dropped the binoculars on the seat. He ran toward the deck, jumped down off the boat and yelled—screamed—for her again.

Kim came up the ladder from the cabin below, ran toward him and jumped down onto the dock, after Charlie.

He was already running for the building and yelled over his shoulder, "Hurry! They're at the restaurant!" He ran around the building for the parking lot and sideswiped a steel barrel, almost lost his footing, and stumbled onto the crushed stone walkway. But he kept moving and jumped in the driver's side of the Suburban. Kim took the corner and he yelled, "We gotta go!"

He already had the vehicle in drive.

"You sure it's them?" she said. She slammed the door after jumping in and grabbed her phone to call for backup.

Chapter 24

THE SHEM CREEK BAR and Grille parking lot was full, the inside crowded with all the people Charlie could see through the windows at the tables. Plenty of heads turned as Charlie and Kim crashed through the entrance holding badges up in front of them.

Kim had called both the U.S. Marshals Office in Charleston and the Mount Pleasant Police, but Charlie said there was no chance they could wait any longer.

They rushed past the bar, the bartender's eyes wide open, watching them as they continued for the glass French doors leading to the outside seating area overlooking Shem Creek.

Just like the front of the building, the wall at the back of the restaurant was mostly glass, giving the patrons a nice view of the sun shining over the creek, but with cool AC instead of the humid outdoor air.

But the view to the outside area was about to provide more than anyone eating lunch had expected.

Charlie reached for the handle on the door to step outside, but for some reason stopped and turned and looked toward the short hall with a RESTROOMS sign above the door with twelve small panes of glass. He could see through to the other side and saw a woman walking toward him from there.

The door opened and out walked the woman he'd last seen blowing him a kiss from the Cessna, flying less than thirty feet over his head at the municipal airport in Tennessee.

Bella Ray didn't see him—not at first—her head down in her phone as she walked toward the doors to go back outside. But she looked up and saw Charlie and Kim, turned and ran in the other direction toward a waitress walking toward her.

Charlie went after her, but Bella Ray shoved the poor waitress into Charlie, knocked someone's lunch off the tray and onto him, covering him with crab chowder and fried clams. Kim tried to go around Charlie but slipped in the chowder on the hardwoods before she could reach for Bella Ray.

But Bella Ray kicked off her high heels and threw them behind her, ran barefoot past the bar and knocked over another restaurant employee as she made it out the front door.

Charlie was up on his feet, made sure the waitress wasn't hurt and went after Bella Ray, past the crowd at the tables and at the bar watching all the commotion.

He turned at the door before he left the restaurant and yelled to Kim, "Don't let Flynn leave... but try to wait." He knew Flynn and whoever else was outside still wouldn't have known they were inside.

Bella Ray ran fast but Charlie was faster. She made it across the parking lot and was about to cross Mill Street when he tackled her onto the strip of grass on the edge of the sidewalk. They both tumbled and rolled, Charlie doing what he could to break their fall and not crush her underneath him.

Cars buzzed by on Mill Street with horns blowing, drivers likely wondering why a man had tackled the attractive young woman with bare feet.

But Charlie didn't pay them any attention, stood up and reached down to help Bella Ray to her feet. He slipped the handcuffs on her before she could say a word. He was breathing heavy—they both were—as he read Bella Ray her rights and escorted her back to the Suburban. He opened the driver's-side door and took the cuff off one of her wrists and latched it to the steering wheel. "You wait here while I go get your boyfriend." He left the door open and let her stand outside with the door open, not wanting her to melt inside the hot Suburban.

"He's not my boyfriend," she yelled and Charlie looked back at her as he opened the door and went inside the restaurant.

He squeezed through the crowd at the door, some trying to leave and others making their way in or waiting for a table. The bar was still full, patrons with a good buzz not about to leave without seeing what else was about to happen.

Kim was at the back door, still inside, and turned to him. "They have no idea," she said. "The three are just sitting there eating."

They both pulled their Glocks and stepped outside, guns raised and pointed at Roger and his friends. "Police!" Charlie yelled. "Roger Flynn, Elizabeth Thornton, you're both under arrest."

Screams filled the outdoor dining area as Charlie and Kim stepped toward the table, their weapons on Roger and Elizabeth.

But a waiter crossed in front of them, seemed to be doing nothing more than trying to get out of their way, and tripped up Kim.

Roger had just enough time to pull a gun from his pants. He turned to the table next to him and grabbed a young woman in a pretty sundress.

She was seated with a young man who tried to pull her back but Roger pointed his gun at him. "Let her go."

The man did as he was told and Roger wrapped his arm around her neck from behind and pointed the gun at her head. He dragged her away from the tables and toward the water.

"Roger!" Charlie yelled. "Let her go. This ends *now*!"

Roger shook his head, nodded with his chin toward Elizabeth and Jason Day. "Get up, you two. Let's go!"

Elizabeth Thornton was up on her feet and already had a gun in her hand she must've been holding under the table.

"Put down your guns," Charlie said.

Elizabeth stepped around Roger and the young woman he had in the crux of his arm.

The man from the table with the young woman pleaded with Roger. "Sir, please... don't hurt my wife. She's... she's pregnant."

Roger pulled the woman closer to the docks, her feet practically dragging on the wood decking below them. He stopped and looked down, his chin on her shoulder. "You're pregnant? You sure? You don't *look* pregnant."

Most of the crowd had disappeared, although cries and whimpers could be heard from those who had ducked behind their tables to hide.

Roger nodded at Charlie and Kim. "You going to put those guns down? Or you really expect me to believe you'd put this poor pregnant mother's life at risk? I can see the headlines now, 'Deputy U.S. Marshal Charlie Harlow shoots and kills again. This time a mother and her unborn child.'" He continued to step back, dragging the young mother with him. He turned to Liz, over his shoulder. "Get in the boat."

Charlie and Kim kept their guns on Roger.

A boat from the Mount Pleasant Police moved slowly toward the dock but Charlie waved it off. "No, back off," he yelled. "Move away... he has a hostage."

The two officers in the boat both looked at each other, then sat down in the boat and turned around and took off down the creek.

Liz turned from Roger and stepped onto the dock, jumped down into the boat and got behind the wheel. She started the engine.

Jason Day had yet to move from the table, his hands up in the air in front of him.

Roger stepped down onto the dock with the young woman. "We're going for a boat ride, mama," he said.

"Please, let her go," cried the young man. The husband, Charlie presumed.

"Convince those two marshals to put their guns away... and I'd say you have a fair chance of seeing your girl again." He grinned. "Assuming she knows how to swim." Roger held the gun on her.

The young man turned to Charlie. "Please..."

Sirens could be heard from the streets. Charlie glanced through the windows and into the restaurant. Police and deputies from the sheriff's office piled inside.

Charlie looked at Kim and gave her a nod. They both lowered their guns and Roger handed the pregnant woman to Elizabeth, easing the woman down onto the boat. Roger hopped down and Elizabeth got behind the wheel. The boat backed away from the dock and they took off down the creek.

Charlie ran for the dock, looking back and forth for a boat he could use.

"Charlie, you can't," Kim said. "He'll kill that young woman."

People had started to come outside, along with the law enforcement officials stepping through the door. The two deputies on the boat pulled up to the dock.

Charlie introduced himself, said to one of the officers, "Any chance you have a helicopter?"

The officer nodded toward one of the deputies. "Sheriff's office does."

Chapter 25

THE HELICOPTER FLEW OVER, heading toward the Hog Island Channel as Kim and Charlie stood up, holding on to the side rails of the boat they were in with the two Mount Pleasant police officers.

Charlie held his hat on his head with his free hand, his eyes ahead at the boat with Roger, the two women and their hostage. "Don't get too close," he said. "I don't want him harming that young woman."

The officer glanced back at Charlie and nodded, turned his eyes back to the water ahead. "We have officers on the shore of the beach. He tries to get around, we'll grab him." He looked up at the helicopter circling back.

Charlie was afraid they were getting too far ahead, and knew the officers had no way of knowing just how slippery Roger was. "This boat go any faster?" he said.

The officer turned to him. "Didn't you just tell me not to get too close?"

Charlie nodded with a grin. "Sorry, I can't let him get away, but I don't want blood on my hands, anything happens to that poor woman."

Up ahead, Roger's boat turned around the southern point of Sullivan's Island.

"What's he doing?" Kim said, almost under her breath, the binoculars up to her face.

Charlie stepped behind Kim on the other side of the boat. "Is the girl all right?"

Kim didn't answer right away, adjusting the binoculars up in front of her eyes. "Oh no," she said. "He's got her out... he's holding her on the edge of the boat."

"The woman?" the officer behind the wheel said.

Kim pulled down the binoculars and turned to Charlie. "He's going to throw her overboard!"

The second officer scrambled around the boat, pulled a life preserver off a hook with the rope in one hand. He put one foot up on the edge of the boat, ready with the life preserver. "Port side," he said to the officer behind the wheel.

Charlie pulled his Glock. "She goes in, I'm taking a shot at Flynn."

Kim handed the binoculars to Charlie. She quickly removed her jacket and shoes and stood port side with the other officer. "What's he doing now?" she said, turning to Charlie.

Charlie had Roger in his view. But then Roger's boat turned out and away from Sullivan's Island at full speed. "What in the hell..."

"Where are they going?" Kim said.

"Oh, shit!" Charlie yelled, seeing Roger through the glass toss the woman off the boat. "He just threw her in the water!" He turned to the officer. "Get this thing moving!"

The officer had the boat moving, full throttle, and Charlie folded his hat and tucked it in his back pocket. He raised his Glock and tried to take aim at Roger, but Elizabeth Thornton knew how to drive a boat, cut it hard and left the young pregnant woman in the boat's wake. They were headed toward the shore.

Charlie didn't have a shot aiming at a boat with a beach behind it, too many people sunbathing on the shore, some in the water... take a chance a stray bullet would strike one of them. He tucked his gun back in the holster.

The officer was getting the boat closer to the young woman who seemed to be struggling to stay afloat; the wake from Roger Flynn's boat had her bobbing up and down and under the water.

Charlie and Kim and the second officer all leaned off the edge of the boat, watching as the woman poked her head up, choking as she tried to scream for help.

They were close to her now, and the officer slowed the boat, getting it close enough for Kim and the officer to jump in and go after her. Kim and the second officer were next to her in the water, helped her hold the life preserver as Charlie pulled the rope toward the boat.

With the help of the officer who'd been driving the boat, they both leaned over and pulled the young woman out of the water, being careful not to hurt her or her baby.

Charlie turned and leaned over again, helped Kim and the second officer up on the ladder. He turned back to the crying woman and wrapped a blanket around her. "You're all right now," he said, glancing at Kim standing next to them, her body drenched in ocean water.

He grabbed the binoculars and watched Roger and Liz, the boat on the south end of the beach and heading right for the shore—until it hit the sand so hard, both of them went flying and hit the deck as it crashed halfway up the beach. But they were up and off the boat and running toward the dunes. Roger appeared to be limping.

A uniformed deputy coming over the dunes and onto the beach ran right past them, Charlie shaking his head wondering why he wouldn't stop them. He assumed the deputy wasn't even sure who he was looking for until the man turned around and started after them.

The officer got the boat as close as he could to the shore. Charlie jumped off into water—up to his waist—and moved his legs as fast as he could with long, slow strides bogged down by his heavy, wet boots. He had his eye on Roger, who stopped on the dune at the back of the beach.

Roger had a gun in his hand and raised it, fired a shot and hit the sheriff's deputy coming up behind him.

The deputy's shoulder kicked back and he collapsed, facedown into the sand.

The beachgoers—men, women, and children—screamed and ran in all directions, the sound of waves crashing between the screams coming after the loud shot from Roger's gun.

Roger and Liz were running and Charlie raised his Glock, thinking maybe he could take a shot. But there were too many people on the beach, running in all directions, nobody looking quite sure where to take cover on a wide-open beach.

He couldn't keep running, and stopped where the deputy lay, the young man's blood soaking into the sand. Charlie knelt down next to him and looked up one more time toward the dunes.

Roger and Liz were gone.

Charlie pulled off his shirt and rolled the deputy over on his back. He saw the wound, right in the man's chest, and used his shirt to put pressure on it, trying to stop the bleeding. "You'll be all right," he said, although he wasn't sure that was the truth. He turned and looked over his shoulder as Kim ran up behind him. "He needs a paramedic!"

And as he said it, the helicopter landed on the beach fifty yards away. Two Mount Pleasant Police officers jumped down onto the sand and ran toward Charlie and the injured deputy.

"He needs to get to the hospital," Charlie said, looking up at the officers as they approached.

One of the two officers said, "I'm a trained EMT." He looked toward the dunes and pointed through the trees. "The parking lot is on the other side of the woods." He nodded in that direction and said to Charlie, "Go get your man. We've got this."

Charlie turned and ran after Roger and Liz, Kim behind him, moving as fast as he could over the dunes and over a wood-planked walkway through a wooded area.

An officer ran toward him, coming from the other direction.

Charlie said, "You see them?"

The officer shrugged, shaking his head. "Just heard the call, a deputy from the sheriff's office is down."

Charlie didn't bother trying to explain or ask any more questions, ran past the officer and toward the parking lot.

He stopped at the end of the walkway and looked around. He didn't see Roger or Liz anywhere, and didn't know which direction to go. He turned to Kim—both of them breathing heavy—and watched people with beach chairs and coolers over their shoulders walking past them to enjoy a day at the beach, unaware of what surrounded them. Police tape would have been handy at that point, he thought. "Might want to get back in your cars," Charlie said to anyone who would listen. But nobody did.

A woman screamed from across the parking lot. "My car! Someone just stole my car!"

Charlie saw a Charleston County sheriff's vehicle pull in, tires squealing, followed by a Charleston County rescue vehicle.

The sheriff, big bellied, stepped out and started running toward them.

But Charlie and Kim didn't wait for him; both ran toward the scream and spotted three teenage girls in bathing suits. "What happened?" he said to the three girls crying, one more hysterical than her friends.

"He had a gun," the hysterical one said. "He took my dad's car! All of our stuff was inside!"

The sheriff came up behind Charlie. "What kind of vehicle was it?"

"It's a Tesla," the girl said. "It's brand new. I wasn't supposed to drive it. My dad's going to kill me when he finds out."

Chapter 26

The sheriff assured Charlie and Kim, "The roads are all blocked. No way they'll get off the island."

"Maybe not with a vehicle," Charlie said. "But you don't know these two. Planes, trains and automobiles."

"But they'll have to cross the bridge," the sheriff said, pulling his sunglasses from his face, cleaning the lenses with a small cloth.

Charlie pulled his wet hat from his back pocket, straightened it out best he could and placed it on his head. "Wouldn't put it past these two to swim across, although it looked to me the old man got hurt when they slammed their boat into the shore."

"Well, rest assured… we have every deputy available and in place," the sheriff said. "All hands are on deck. Twenty-seven total, between my office and the Mount Pleasant PD."

"With all due respect," Charlie said, "I'm not sure we doubled that number it'd be enough. Roger's slippery as an eel."

Charlie and the sheriff both looked up at the helicopter coming over the trees from the beach. The sheriff said, "He shot one of my men. I assure you as God is my judge, that man's not getting off this island."

Charlie gave Kim a nod. "We'd better get back to our vehicle, make sure Bella Ray didn't gnaw her arm off."

The sheriff gave Charlie and Kim a ride back to the Shem Creek Bar and Grille and Charlie stepped out, hurried over to the Suburban, Bella Ray in the driver's seat with the door wide open, her long legs hanging over the side. Her makeup had run down with the sweat dripping from her face.

"You can't just leave someone handcuffed outside in the heat like that," Bella Ray said, trying to yank her arm from Charlie's grasp as he unlocked the handcuff from the steering wheel.

He turned her around and cuffed both wrists together, opened the back door and pushed her into the rear passenger seat. He locked both doors and got in front, started the engine and had the AC cranking on high, although it was mostly hot, stale air with the smell of spent marijuana blowing out from the vents. He looked at Bella Ray through the rearview mirror. "I'm sure this heat is nothing compared to what Jack felt when you and Roger lit him on fire down there in that basement."

Charlie turned and looked back at Bella Ray over his shoulder. "You going to tell us what Roger's end game is? What he's been after? Or are you going to continue trying to play you're just the innocent victim caught up in something you know nothing about?"

She stared back at him without answering.

Charlie looked toward the entrance to the restaurant where Kim stood, just outside the door with three officers. Jason Day was in handcuffs.

"So what's this guy Jason Day's deal?" Charlie said, his eyes back in the rearview mirror.

Bella Ray turned and looked out the back passenger-side window. "He knew Jack," she said.

"I know that. But what's his deal? Why'd Roger come down here? He got something you three are looking for?"

She kept her eyes to her right, out the back passenger window, and didn't answer Charlie.

"So you're not going to talk? Then let me guess," Charlie said. "I've been on a wild goose chase... playing cat-and-mouse with the three of you. And I'm guessing the only reason nobody left the country, or the Southeast, for that matter, is because Jack left some money—probably a lot of it—somewhere around Charleston. But nobody knows exactly where it is." He turned, looked at Bella Ray. "Am I about right?" He kept his gaze on her, but she wouldn't turn to look at him. "Is that what sent you all out to Tennessee? Jack's cousin knew something about where Jack had hid the money? Billy Thornton the one pointed you in the right direction?" Charlie thought for a moment.

Bella Ray stared back at him. "I had nothing to do with killing Jack, you know."

Charlie huffed out a laugh. "I don't know if you did or you didn't. It'll be someone else's job to figure that out. But you did a good job leading me away from the house, didn't you? I'm still not sure how you all pulled it off. Jack leaves with Liz, goes all the way to the airport but somehow he ends up back at your house? Was it Roger? Takes Jack back there for the money he thought was in that safe? And when it's not..."

"I didn't know Roger was going to kill Jack."

Charlie looked at her through the rearview. "What'd you think he was going to do? Just come out and ask Jack for the money?" He looked out the window toward Kim and the officers with Jason Day. "I shouldn't have been so foolish myself, should've locked you up just for whacking me on the head with that shovel."

Charlie pushed open the door and stepped down from the Suburban. He opened the back door and reached in, pulled Bella Ray outside and led her by the arm to one of the sheriff's deputies. "Deputy?" he said. "You got someplace you can hold this young lady for a little while?"

The deputy nodded. "I can put her in a holding cell at the office if—"

"Whatever you do will be great," Charlie said. "But do us all a favor and don't take those cuffs off her. Not even if she *is* in a cell."

The deputy led her to one of the cruisers and put her in back.

Charlie gave Kim a quick glance, then walked to the Suburban, raised the rear hatch and lifted the rug. He reached in and pulled out his Remington 700 sniper rifle, held it down by his side and slammed the hatch closed. He stepped back over to Kim with Jason Day and the two officers. "He claim total innocence?" Charlie said. "Doesn't know a thing about what these three were up to?" He had his eyes on Jason. "You going to try and claim you weren't even aware you were dining with a wanted man?"

Kim said, "He said he'll cooperate, as long as his lawyer's present."

Charlie squinted his eyes and stared back at the good-looking, middle-aged man. "You haven't been arrested or technically even charged as of yet. Therefore, I wouldn't say you'd need a lawyer present just to tell us what you know about what Roger and your dead friend's ex-wife are up to now."

Jason, well-dressed in khaki shorts and a golf shirt, shook his head, staring right back into Charlie's eyes. "I won't talk to you or anybody else without my lawyer. I know my rights."

Charlie nodded slowly, pulling at his chin. "That's good to know," he said. He took a step closer to Jason, got right up in his face. He spoke in a hushed tone. "Here's the thing..." Charlie paused and looked around. "You cooperate, you have nothing to worry about. Because, I don't want you, Mr. Day. I could care less about you and your oversized home and your boats..." He looked away, toward the road. "All I want is Roger Flynn."

Jason kept his gaze on Charlie. He didn't look intimidated by Charlie in any way.

"And you're aware Roger Flynn is wanted for killing your friend, Jack Thornton? And he didn't just shoot him, you know. He burned him to a point beyond recognition. Needed dental records to—"

"Roger said he didn't kill him," Jason said.

Charlie fixed his hat back on his head. "Well, what did you expect him to tell you? He needed you on his side... I assume to tell him where to find whatever it is he's looking for. Which, if I were to make an educated guess, is likely a hell of a lot of cash Jack must've stashed away somewhere for his planned escape to wherever he was going."

Jason looked away. "I've said enough. I want my lawyer."

Charlie felt his face start to burn not only from the hot sun beating down on them, but from somewhere inside. He had had enough of Jack Thornton and Roger Flynn and all their friends.

Charlie glanced in through the front door and into the empty restaurant. The place had been closed, everyone asked to leave; the parking lot blocked with wood barriers the police had put up. He gave Kim a look. "We'll be right back." Charlie opened the front door and grabbed Jason by the arm, yanked him inside the restaurant.

Inside, a man—the owner of the Shem Creek Bar and Grille—stood behind the front desk and looked up at Charlie. "Officer, please. I need to open my restaurant. I'm sorry, but I'm losing money every minute I can't have customers in here."

Charlie nodded. "I understand. But if you'd just give me a minute, we'll let you open up again real soon." He pulled Jason Day toward the men's room, the man's feet tripping over themselves with Charlie practically dragging him backward over the tile floor.

Charlie kicked open the bathroom door, the Remington 700 down by his side. He let go of Jason and turned to lock the door.

Jason looked scared, shaking his head. "What the... what the hell are you—"

Charlie grabbed Jason by the back of his head, a clump of hair in his hand, and stuck the shotgun barrel in Jason's mouth. "Now you listen to me, you piece of shit. Roger Flynn not only killed Jack Thornton but also, very likely, a young deputy down there on that beach. He blew up my car... and he damn near had my wife executed. I can see to it you walk away from this with your hands clean. Or I can see to it you're tried as an accomplice in—at the very least— harboring a wanted man and aiding his escape. Not to mention, that deputy dies... I'll make sure the judge and jury know you played a substantial role in his murder. You're looking at twenty years, at least. And I don't care what kind of slick lawyer you have by your side." He held the barrel in Jason's mouth for a moment longer, then gave a gentle nod with his chin and pulled the barrel out. "Now. Are you ready to talk?"

Chapter 27

CHARLIE WALKED OUT OF the restaurant with his hand on Jason Day's arm. Kim was standing by the Suburban, a phone up to her ear. She glanced at him and said into the phone, "He's right here. He just walked out." She held the phone toward Charlie. "It's Frank."

Charlie turned Jason around and took the handcuffs off his wrists. "Tell Frank I'll call him back."

Kim shook her head, kept her arm extended toward Charlie with the phone in her hand. "He wants to talk to you."

Charlie rolled his eyes and took the phone. "Frank, I've got Jason Day right here in front of me, and he claims to know where Roger Flynn and Liz Thornton'll be heading if they happen to get off the island." He held the phone down away from his mouth and said to Jason, "You're not free to go yet, in case that's what you were wondering." He nodded toward Kim. "Don't let him go anywhere." He stepped away from the two, put the phone back up to his ear. "Frank? You there?"

"Yeah, I'm here, Charlie. You need me to come down there? Or you and Kim close to wrapping this thing up?"

Charlie removed his hat and wiped the sweat from his brow. "You can come down and help out if you'd like, but I'm hoping it'll end up being a waste of gas for you."

"I don't pay for my own gas, Charlie. I'm just interested in one thing right now and that's—"

"We got a couple dozen deputies and plenty of police officers down here... a couple US deputy marshals from the Charleston office. On top of it, some other people helping out I'm not even sure where they came from. I think we'll be all right without you."

"But you don't have him in custody yet. I've told you this enough times... don't count your chickens until they're hatched, Charlie. I just... I don't know what it is, how a sixty-something-year-old man can continue to slip out of your—"

"Frank, you let me off the phone, maybe I can get back to it." Charlie eyeballed Jason Day, standing next to Kim without either one saying a word. "I got his friend here—Jack Thornton's friend, actually—Jason Day told me Roger's trying to locate a bag of cash Jack had stashed down this way. That's why he went to Tennessee. Apparently Jack's cousin played more of a role than we suspected and sent Roger down this way."

Frank said, "You mean the cousin who told you he didn't know a thing about it?"

"Yeah, he'll have to be dealt with at some point," Charlie said. "But apparently Jack made a lot of trips down here over the years. Turns out, according to Mr. Day, he's got a girlfriend somewhere in the area, in the town of Mount Pleasant." He glanced over at Kim, gave her a nod to say he'd be another minute.

"I assume you've got a name?" Frank said.

"As soon as you let me off the phone we're going to go find her. Roger and Liz were planning to go see her after the lunch they were having with Mr. Day. We interrupted that."

Frank went quiet for a moment. "I hope this isn't another dead end, Charlie. Seems to be that's all there is with this guy."

"Well, let's hope that's not the case. Only so many dead-ends you can run into before luck turns your way."

"Let's hope so," Frank said. "Keep me updated."

Charlie hung up and walked back to Kim, handed her the phone. He looked Jason Day in the eye. "You'd better be telling us the truth," he said. "Or I'll see to it whatever comes down on Roger comes down just as hard on you."

Jason glanced at Kim, then back to Charlie. "I told you everything I know."

Charlie thought for a moment, gave Jason a nod. "All right, you're free to go."

Kim said, "He's free to go? What? Why would we—"

Charlie headed for the Suburban. "I'll explain on the way." He reached for the knob on the door and pulled it open without looking back. "Looks like Bella Ray wasn't Jack Thornton's only girlfriend. Had another flavor down here... seemed to do a good job of keeping it quiet for the ten years they've been together."

"She's here?"

Charlie and Kim both stepped inside the Suburban, Charlie turning the key in the ignition. He looked straight ahead where Jason Day had been standing a moment earlier but had already disappeared. He handed Kim a piece of paper. "Here's the address."

"Did you let the sheriff know?" she said.

Charlie backed away from the curb and cut the wheel, spun the big vehicle around and headed for the exit. He said, "We don't need all the commotion over there just yet. Let him keep his men where they are." He could feel Kim watching him but kept his eyes on the road until he turned to her. "*What?*"

"You really think it's smart, just the two of us go over there? I hate to say it, but we haven't exactly been living up to our so-called reputations with this one."

Charlie nodded, tapped the location into the GPS built right into the dashboard.

"Laurel Lakes?" she said. "What's that, the community she lives in?"

Charlie shrugged. "I assume so."

"No house number?"

"Just the street name in Laurel Lakes, is what Mr. Day told me. He didn't know the number. But he said it's a one-story home, tan stucco exterior. Drives a black BMW, keeps it in the driveway."

"And you really don't think we should let the sheriff know?"

Charlie looked at the GPS, followed it off Ben Sawyer Boulevard until it told him to turn right onto Rifle Range Road. "Go ahead and give the sheriff a call then," he said. "Just let him know to be on the lookout for a black BMW sedan in the Laurel Lakes area. He sees it out there on the road, she either got away from us or she's on her way back."

Charlie pulled over in front of the house that matched the description Jason Day had given him. The black BMW was in the driveway. He leaned toward Kim enough so he could see out her window and up toward the house. "Looks quiet," he said. "So far."

He grabbed the Remington from the back seat and stepped out from the car with it, walked up the stone-paved walkway to the oversized door, like something that belonged on a castle. He looked around the yard and toward the strip of palm trees planted between Jack's girlfriend's house and the neighbor's.

Charlie knocked on the door and felt the thickness of it with his knuckles. He turned to glance at Kim, two steps behind him.

They both stood quiet.

The latch clicked and the bolt slid inside it. The door opened, and a pretty, middle-aged woman with long, gray hair stood looking out at them. She had a paperback in her hand, held open to the page she was reading. She removed the glasses on the edge of her nose and let them hang from the diamond-like chain around her neck. Her eyes opened wide as she glanced down at the shotgun Charlie held down by his side.

He held out his badge. "I'm Deputy U.S. Marshal Charlie Harlow." He nodded toward Kim. "This is Deputy U.S. Marshal Kim Rivers. Are you Gina Matthews?"

"U.S. Marshals?" she said. She again looked at the Remington, appearing calm and relaxed. "This must be some serious business?" She looked from Charlie to Kim.

Charlie nodded. "We're looking for two people you may or may not be expecting. Do you know and have you seen Mr. Roger Flynn? He's with a woman I'm sure you know well, Mrs. Elizabeth Thornton?"

Gina Matthews turned and reached behind the wall, Charlie almost raised the shotgun, but her hand came back with a glass of wine. She took a sip.

She stepped outside and let the storm door close behind her. She remained quiet, taking a sip from her glass with her eyes on Charlie from over the rim. "Why would I be expecting Roger?"

"Roger Flynn and your boyfriend's ex-wife," Kim said. "Are you saying you haven't seen them?"

She shook her head. "Why would I?"

"Well, they're here," Charlie said. "In Mount Pleasant. Shot a deputy on the beach... abducted a young pregnant woman and threw her off the boat. We've got the area covered with a couple-dozen law enforcement officials. He's not getting off the island. And from what I understand his plan was to come here."

Kim Matthews had looked relaxed and calm as a cucumber at first, but that act seemed to dissipate. "Roger is here? In Mount Pleasant? Oh my God," she said. "Do you think they're—"

"It's my understanding you have something they want, which I assume is the cash Jack hid down here, whether it was with you or—"

"I don't have any of Jack's money. I... I mean, I don't have anything they're looking for. I swear to you." Her relaxed look had completely disappeared, replaced with nerves she wasn't able to hide.

Kim said, "Ma'am, we're not only here to hopefully take Roger and Elizabeth into custody, who've been on the run for quite a few days at this point... but we're here to also protect you if we need to. But we're just hoping you're willing to cooperate and tell us what you know."

"We're not judge or jury, ma'am," Charlie said. "But if you do have something that doesn't belong to you—something Jack might've left with you or somewhere in the area—I suggest you tell us where it is. All we ask is you don't play any games with us. Not now. Your life may depend on us."

Chapter 28

CHARLIE WAS OUT IN the street talking with the sheriff and a sergeant from the Mount Pleasant PD, both apologizing for letting Roger and Elizabeth get away.

"I warned you both they were slippery," Charlie said. "But we're going to get them this time. I feel good about it." He looked up toward Gina's house with the garage door open, Kim pulling Gina's black BMW into the garage and out of sight. "They'll show up here sooner or later." He turned and glanced around the yard and through the trees surrounding the house. "I just don't know when."

The sheriff shifted his stance. "What makes you so sure they're not just hiding out, waiting, expecting things'll clear if they stay out of sight long enough?"

"I think Roger Flynn's waited long enough. He wants the money he believes belongs to him. And he's done waiting around."

"You seem confident," the sergeant said.

Charlie grinned. "So far I've read Roger Flynn like a book. Just can't flip the pages fast enough. I'm just hoping this time I'm the one who's a step ahead, not two steps back, the way it's been so far."

The sheriff straightened his hat. "We'll help you however we can, Charlie. I just don't want to pull my men from the roads and bridges unless I—"

"Well, we've got it covered here for now," Charlie said, looking back at the house. "We just need to keep everybody out of sight, not let them know we're all here when they finally show up. Just have your teams ready." He nodded and turned to walk away. "I do appreciate it."

He headed back up the driveway toward the house, adjusting the bulletproof vest he always found uncomfortable, but wasn't going to take any chances. He walked through the front door and into the kitchen.

Kim was leaning against the counter, Gina Matthews at the table with a cup of tea in front of her. It looked like she hadn't touched it.

Charlie stood over the table and looked down at Gina. "Now, I just need to be clear one more time," he said, "and make sure you understand that once we recover the money, it's going to be confiscated by the U.S. Marshals Service. Your chances of holding on to even a penny of it are slim. So you might as well tell us where it is."

She looked up at him and shook her head. "I told you, I don't *know* where it is. Jack was supposed to call me, let me know where to pick it up. But he never called, for obvious reasons."

Kim straightened up from the edge of the counter. "Miss Matthews, we've tried to make it clear the U.S. Marshals Service isn't here to decide whether or not you're involved or what you were involved in or, frankly, what kind of relationship you had with Jack Thornton. We're here to bring Roger and Elizabeth to justice and maybe stop them from hurting you. What happens after they're in custody is, for the most part, out of our hands. But as we've explained, all you have to do is cooperate."

Charlie stood quiet, looking down at Gina, but she no longer had the look of a woman concerned for her life. He glanced out the window and into the woods behind the house. "Are you sure you're the only person they believe knows where this money's supposed to be?"

Gina started to nod. "Jack didn't trust many people. But he trusted me. He always knew he could. In fact, he always wondered aloud which one of his friends would turn on him. I don't believe he ever thought it would be Roger, but most people will do anything for money... as sad as that sounds."

"Bet he had no idea Bella Ray was going to turn on him?"

Gina shrugged. "You know, we both had an agreement we could do what we wanted when we weren't together.

I didn't think he'd latch on to her the way he did, but he was starting to question how much he trusted her."

"Then why didn't he just get out of there? You and he take off? Especially since he had no intention of hanging around for the trial."

Gina Matthews stared back at Charlie and didn't answer his question. She got up from the table and stood over the sink, looking out into the backyard. "Jack wanted me to go with him."

"Go where?" Kim said.

Gina turned from the window. "To Mexico. That was his plan."

"Why didn't you just go?" Charlie said.

Gina stared back at Charlie, taking a moment before she replied. "I didn't want to live my life on the run. And I'm not sure I wanted to disappear forever the way he was going to have to."

"I imagine he had plenty of money," Charlie said. "I'm sure you could've made it work." He cracked a crooked grin. "I'm going to guess, based on what I've heard, there's two-to-three million dollars out there... wherever it is."

She held her gaze on Charlie. "Like I said, I didn't want to be on the run. And I have family here. My sister's here. I couldn't leave her all alone."

Charlie stepped out from the kitchen and into the room at the front of the house. He pulled the curtains aside and looked out toward the street. It was just about dusk, the sun on its way down but still plenty of light left in the day. He walked back into the kitchen. "You said you have a sister? She live around here?"

Gina nodded. "A little under twenty minutes from here, has a small house she owns on the other side of the Wando River."

Charlie thought for a moment, had a look on his face as he glanced at Kim who was looking back at him like she knew he had something on his mind. He said to Gina, "Any chance Roger or Elizabeth know about her?"

"My sister?" Gina said. Then her expression dropped from her face, her mouth open as if she wanted to speak but it took a moment for anything to come out. "I... I don't know. I mean, they probably know I have a sister, but..."

Charlie's wheels were turning and he took a step closer to Gina, still standing in front of the sink with her eyes down toward the floor. He grabbed her arm but she still wouldn't look up at him "Gina? Listen to me. You have to tell me the truth." He said, "Would you please look at me?"

She finally lifted her gaze to his.

Charlie said, "Does your sister have Jack's money? Is that where he hid it? Is that money at your sister's house?"

Gina pulled her arm away and sat down at the table, her head rested in her hands, elbows down. She looked up at Charlie. "Do you... do you think he'll go to her house looking for it?"

Charlie said, "Are you telling me that's where it is? At your sister's house?"

Gina nodded.

Charlie looked at Kim. "We need to get someone over there, right away. Get the sheriff on the horn." He grabbed the corded phone from the wall and handed the handset to Gina. "You gotta call your sister. Right now."

Kim's hands were shaking as she took the phone from Charlie and pushed the buttons. Her eyes went from Charlie to Kim and back down to the phone in her hand as she lifted it to her ear. She shook her head. "She's not answering."

"Are you calling her house?" Charlie said.

"I'm calling her cell. She doesn't have a landline anymore."

"But is she—"

She started to leave a message and held her index finger up toward Charlie, gesturing for him to wait. "Hey, it's me," she said. "I need you to call me back right away, as soon as you get this. Please... call me back right away." Kim held the phone in her hand, but her finger on the switch.

"She typically return your calls right away?" Charlie said.

She stared at him. "She usually answers her phone, no matter what she's doing. It's always in her hand."

Charlie could see her swallow, her nerves clearly getting the best of her.

The phone in her hand rang and she jumped, held her hand over her heart and answered. "Lucy?" Her eyes went to Charlie. She gasped and started to shake her head. "No... no... please. No. What have you done with my sister?"

Charlie reached his hand out. "Is it Roger?"

Kim nodded and held her hand over the mouthpiece. "He said if I don't tell him where the money is... my sister will die."

Charlie took the phone from her. "Roger?"

But Roger had already hung up.

Chapter 29

CHARLIE STOOD IN THE driveway on the phone with Frank, the driveway filled with sheriff's vehicles and half a dozen Mount Pleasant squad cars. "Yes, you heard me right," he said. "He's holding the sister hostage, said he wants the money, and Gina Matthews finally admitted she knew Jack hid it up in the attic."

"At the sister's house?"

"Yes," Charlie said. "But the sister doesn't even know it's up there."

"And we don't know if Roger knows exactly where Jack hid it?"

Charlie looked around. "No, we don't. And you know the risk is he figures it out, takes the money and kills the sister in the process."

Frank was quiet on the other end. "Or he holds on to her knowing she may be the only way he'll get out of there... the threat of killing her if we don't let him leave."

"There's no way I'm letting him get away this time, Frank." He looked around at all the law enforcement officials, all the men and women standing around... waiting. Charlie knew Roger still had the upper hand. "So you want to make the call, Frank? We wait any longer..."

Frank said, "I think you go over there, get Roger on the phone from outside—right there in front of the house—tell him where the money is. At this point, we have to focus on getting the woman free, stop him from killing her. And once you know she's safe, you do what you have to do to apprehend Roger Flynn. In fact, I'm not even sure I care about Thornton's ex-wife at this point. We want Roger Flynn." Frank paused. "Shit, I should've gone down there with you."

Charlie hung up the phone and slipped it in his pocket. He turned as all conversations between law enforcement officials stopped... their attention on Charlie.

The sheriff walked over to him, thumbs hooked in his belt. "Well?" he said. "What do you want to do?"

Charlie paused a moment before he spoke. "Well, we're going to go over there and surround the house. But I'm going to need everyone to stay out of sight, just like we were doing here. Roger's not stupid. He'll know we're all out there. But I don't want to make him panic, cause him to do something we'll all regret." He turned around to Gina, her arms folded across her chest, staring back at him and clearly shaken by the predicament she'd put her sister in. "Miss Matthews?" he said. "When we get over there, we're going to get on the phone with Roger, tell him exactly where the money is. But it'll be on the condition he lets your sister go."

Gina started to speak but stopped, almost appeared to be hesitant with Charlie's plan.

He gave her a look. "Miss Matthews? You have something you need to say?"

Gina Matthews started to cry, wiping a tear from her cheek. "There's a problem," she said. "The money... it's not all there."

"The money's not all *where*? At the house?" He stared back at Kim, rubbed the stubble on his face and looked off in another direction. "You mind clarifying exactly what you're trying to say?"

She nodded. "It's... the money is only half of what Roger thinks Jack hid down here."

Charlie kept his eyes on Gina, but she turned her gaze down toward the ground. "He knows exactly how much there's supposed to be? You mean, you tell him it's up there, he'll know something's missing?"

Gina stared into Charlie's eyes and nodded.

He took off his hat and smacked it against his hip. "Shit," he said. He turned to Kim, standing a few feet away with one of the deputy marshals from the Charleston office. "Roger's travelled by car, by train, plane, boat... and by foot to get what he's been after. I have a feeling he's not going to grab and run without double-checking to make sure he's got exactly what he came for." Charlie ran his hand through his hair and left it there for a moment, looking up toward Gina's house.

Kim stepped toward him and took him by the arm. "Can I talk to you for a second?" She pulled him away from Gina and the other deputies.

The two walked off and stood under a large live oak halfway down the driveway. Charlie looked back to make sure Gina Matthews wasn't going to do anything foolish, like try to run with a few dozen officers in the area. "Are you really afraid he sees there's only half, he's going to—"

"Kill the sister?" he said, nodding. "This guy's not all right up there. I could see him making this into a real scene, kill the girl right there in front of everybody just to make his point."

Kim looked toward the street. "Then what if we just wait?" she said. "We don't tell Roger the money's in the attic."

"Then what? Negotiate with a sociopathic killer like he's some kind of a normal person? Besides, the chance is good he's going to find it on his own anyway once they start searching, realize it's not all there. Gina said it's a small house." He took a deep breath and looked up, the Remington still in his hand, by his side. "I say we go over and I try to get him in my sights. If I've got a shot... I'm taking it."

Charlie was behind the wheel and Kim next to him in the passenger seat, her Glock out on her lap as they pulled up the driveway. Gina was in the back seat looking past Charlie and Kim toward the sister's house.

A rust-colored Chrysler LeBaron with a broken tail light was parked in front of the one-car garage door with peeled paint.

The grass in the small yard was in need of a good cut, the tiny ranch home's white vinyl siding stained with green mildew.

Charlie turned off the engine and removed the key from the ignition, stepped down from the Suburban and opened the rear passenger door. He grabbed his Remington from behind the driver's seat and glanced at Gina. "Keep your head down," he said, wondering if it would have made more sense to leave her with one of the deputies.

Kim came around from the passenger side, her Glock in her hand by her side.

They walked toward the Chrysler, but Charlie stopped right behind the trunk when he heard something inside. He turned to Kim. "You hear that?"

Kim stood still, her ear turned, and nodded. She raised her gun toward the trunk's lid and held it there.

Charlie looked up at the house, ran his eyes along the windows expecting to see Roger, or possibly Gina looking out at them. Charlie would love to take a shot, had the Remington ready, grasping it with both hands. But he stepped to the driver's side of the LeBaron and opened the door. He reached around the floor for a trunk latch but couldn't find one and looked through the windshield at the house. He didn't like how quiet and empty it seemed.

He reached around the steering wheel, felt a set of keys and pulled them from the ignition. He walked back to the trunk, his finger on the Remington's trigger, and slid the key in the lock. He had the shotgun raised—Kim with her Glock next to him—and turned the key.

The trunk lifted with Charlie and Kim pointing their guns inside.

A man and woman, both far too big and maybe a bit on the heavy side to be shoved into a trunk, were squeezed together and tied up with rope... their mouths covered with duct tape.

Charlie reached in his back pocket for his knife, opened the blade and leaned toward the woman. She had a look of fear in her eyes, trying to scream behind the tape, shaking her round head.

"I'm not going to hurt you," Charlie said, pointing to the badge on his belt. "U.S. Marshals Service." He held up the knife to show her. "I'm just cutting you free."

Kim and Charlie helped the woman get out from the trunk, although she had a hard time getting her legs over the edge and almost fell to the ground, but Charlie caught her by the arm before she landed.

The man inside with the woman appeared to have been beaten up, his eyes badly swollen, with blood mixed in and sweat covering his ghost-white, chubby face.

"You all right, sir?" Charlie said, removing the tape from the man's mouth. He cut the rope and helped the man get out from the trunk.

Both the man and woman looked around. "Where are we?"

Charlie took the keys from the trunk's lock and held them up. "This your car?"

The man nodded, then turned to hug his wife. They both had tears coming down their faces.

Charlie said, "You might want to get in that car, get out of here." He nodded to Kim and handed her his own set of keys from his pocket. "You mind backing the Suburban out of their way?"

The man said to Charlie, "An older man and a woman got in the trunk with my wife, held a gun to her head and made me drive them off the island to get beyond the officers on the bridge." He looked around. "They knocked me around pretty good, made me get in the trunk with her as soon as we crossed."

Charlie gave him a gentle push toward the driver's door and wiped his hand after feeling the soaked-through sweat on the man's back. "Go on, get in your car and get out of here. You know where the Mount Pleasant Police Station is?"

The man nodded.

"Drive on over there, explain to them everything that happened. They'll take care of you."

The woman made her way to the passenger side and looked across the roof.

"Go!" Charlie said. "Get out of here, before one of you gets killed."

They both scrambled and got inside the car, started the engine and backed out so fast they nearly took out Kim stepping down from the Suburban she'd pulled off onto the grass. The tires squealed as they hit the grass, a cloud of smoke coming out from the tailpipe.

Chapter 30

CHARLIE AND KIM STOOD behind the Suburban, watching the front door knowing Roger was somewhere in the house watching them. Neither one of them thought knocking would make much sense... Charlie having visions of what happened to Deputy Ted Moore.

They hadn't heard much of a sound, other than a car or two driving by on the street behind them.

The police officers and the sheriff's deputies had surrounded the area but stayed far enough away, as Charlie had asked them to, so Roger wouldn't be threatened as much if he saw them out there. Although Charlie had a feeling Roger knew it wasn't just he and Kim outside waiting for him.

Charlie curled the bill of his hat with one hand, pulled the hat down tight on his head. "You ready?" he said, giving Kim a nod. They both hurried, covered in full tactical gear, and ran up the front steps, turned and leaned their backs against the house on either side of the front door.

Charlie pounded on the door with the side of his fist. "Roger Flynn? You in there? This is Deputy U.S. Marshal Charlie Harlow." He again pounded on the door. "You come out here now... or we're coming in to get you."

He hadn't taken the door ram with him but wished he had. So instead he stepped in front of the door and pointed the barrel of the Remington 700 at the knob and pulled the trigger. The rifle exploded and left a splintered hole the size of a nickel between the knob and the frame. Charlie planted his right foot and used his boot to kick the door open He kept the rifle raised in front of him.

Kim walked in behind him and the two looked around the messy living room, with empty cans of beer and magazines spread all over the pine coffee table in front of the couch.

"Roger!" Charlie yelled. "I don't want any surprises," he said. "I'd appreciate you come out here with your hands raised up above your head." He was careful with each step, stayed behind the wall but stuck his head through the open doorway into the kitchen.

It was quiet.

At least until a shot was fired from down the hall on the right.

It barely missed Charlie and took a good chunk from the wall just over his head. Bits and pieces of plaster and wood fell onto his head and shoulders. He threw himself back behind the wall in the living room and sat, with Kim on the other side of the doorway, thinking through his next move.

"We can't take a shot," Kim said. "Not with Gina's sister in here."

Charlie nodded, crouching on the floor, holding his rifle. "He'll use her as a shield." He turned toward the doorway and poked just enough of his head out to make sure Roger could hear him. "Roger! It's over now. Let the girl go." He shifted his feet and tried to look down the hall.

Another shot was fired, but it came from somewhere on the left. He tried to look without getting his head shot off, poked his head out just enough to see an open door next to the refrigerator on the far wall.

Kim stuck her head out to take a look toward the left where the second shot came from. "The garage," she said. She got up on her feet, her back pressed against the wall, and raised her Glock toward the door leading to the garage. But the half step she took from the doorway was a half step too much.

A third shot was fired and Kim dropped her Glock as she fell to the floor. She held her leg. "Shit," she said. Blood came through her pants.

Charlie could see the pain on her face, looked at the blood on the linoleum and leaned his Remington against the wall. He pulled her away from the doorway and dragged her to the other side of the couch, away from the doorway to the kitchen and the back of the house. He picked up her Glock and handed it to her. He crouched down in front of her, put his hand on her shoulder. "Can you hang in there?" he said.

Kim nodded, but Charlie wasn't buying it. There was a lot of blood.

"We gotta get you out of here," he said.

She removed the magazine from her Glock and slid it back in. "I'm fine," she said. "Take a shot at that door leading to the garage," she said. "One of them's in there."

He shook his head. "Who knows if the sister's down the hall or in that garage. I can't take that chance." He looked at the hole in her pants covered in blood. "We gotta back off, Kim. You're hurt." He had his two-way on his vest, pressed the button and announced an officer had been shot. He reached down for her, lifted her to her feet and tried to take as much of her weight onto him as he could. He grabbed his rifle and held it with one hand, carried Kim through the front door and out to the Suburban. He saw a couple of deputies moving closer but waiting behind the old live oaks on the other side of the street.

He helped Kim into the passenger seat of the Suburban. "Stay down," he said, looking toward the garage. He looked into the back seat at Gina, crouched down on the floor between the seats with her arms over her head.

He closed Kim's door and stayed low, his rifle raised toward the house.

A shot was fired from somewhere inside and hit the front left fender of the Suburban, no more than a foot or two from Charlie. He ran around to the driver's side and opened the door. He ducked inside, his head behind the dash, and started the engine. He turned up the AC to keep Kim comfortable.

"We can't run from him," she said, her voice cracking with agony.

Charlie shook his head. "We're not." He lifted his head and looked over the back seat toward the driveway and the road behind them. Two sheriff's vehicles pulled in with lights flashing. Six Mount Pleasant police officers armed and in tactical gear came through the trees from the neighbors' yards.

A deputy pulled open the passenger door and Charlie helped him carry Kim to the deputy's vehicle behind them.

"Get her right to the hospital," Charlie said. He looked Kim in the eye with his hand about to close the door. "You take care of yourself."

He slammed the door closed and looked toward the house. He wasn't sure, but thought he heard a car's engine start on the other side of the garage door. He lifted the Remington with both hands and ran toward the house.

But he'd only taken four steps when the garage door smashed into pieces, a Chevy Blazer crashing through in reverse, sending splinters and broken door panels flying through the air at Charlie.

The rear end of the Chevy Blazer sped straight at him but he dove out of the way. He dropped his rifle when he hit the ground, but pulled the Glock from his belt, rolled his body and fired six shots at the Blazer, rolling in the tall grass trying to straighten out, half the garage door stuck on the vehicle's roof rack.

Bullets were fired from inside the Blazer.

Charlie ran around to the back side of the Suburban to take cover. The deputies and officers did the same, ducking or diving for behind their vehicles.

Charlie watched Elizabeth Thornton inside the Blazer, her shaved head popping up from behind the passenger door with both hands stuck out the open window. She fired a few shots, one after the other, without taking aim at anything, hitting more of the trees around them than anything else. Roger did the same, one hand on the steering wheel, the other firing his gun out the window at whatever and whoever was in front of them.

Charlie got to his feet and ran toward the Blazer as it smashed into the side of a Mount Pleasant officer's vehicle. He took aim at Roger and fired two shots. Roger's gun fell from his hand and bounced on the driveway. Charlie fired another shot and the Blazer jetted across the road and smashed into a maple tree in the middle of a neighbor's yard on the other side.

Both Blazer doors opened. Roger and Elizabeth both fell out to the ground, faces covered in blood, and got up to try and run. Roger had a severe limp and was unarmed. Elizabeth turned with one gun still in her hand, firing shots toward Charlie but not coming close.

One of the deputies stepped out from behind his vehicle, from no more than fifteen feet away, and fired a shot... hit Elizabeth right in the chest. She took another shot herself and tried to fire toward the deputy. But she stumbled and fell to the ground with her next and final step.

Charlie ran as fast as he could at Roger, who wasn't moving well at all but tried to grab the gun Liz had dropped. Before Roger could reach for it, Charlie tackled him onto the grass. Roger went down easy and Charlie felt like he'd taken down nothing but a frail old man.

He grabbed Roger's arm and twisted it. He turned Roger onto his stomach and slipped the cuffs on his wrist without saying a word. He yanked Roger by his arms and lifted him to his feet, handing him to one of the officers. "Go ahead, read him his rights," Charlie said. "But don't go anywhere. He's coming with me." He turned and hurried to the Chevy Blazer and looked inside the back seat.

Gina Matthew's sister wasn't there.

Charlie ran across the street, passing by the dozens of law enforcement officials coming from behind their cars, from the back of the house, and wherever else they'd been hiding around the property. He pulled open the back door to the Suburban. But Gina wasn't there. He turned to one of the deputies. "Where'd she go?"

The deputy looked at him, shaking his head like he didn't know who he was talking about.

"Gina!" he yelled. "Gina Matthews! Where'd you go?" He looked around the yard and ran through the front door and into the house. He stepped over the puddle of blood and into the kitchen, turning to his right down the hall. A ladder had been pulled down from the small square hole in the ceiling. He put one foot on the rung and looked up into the attic, the only light a single bulb hanging from the rafters he could see through the opening. "Gina? You up there?"

Nobody answered. He turned and hurried back to the kitchen, and by the door to the backyard were a few bills scattered along the tall grass, but he didn't see anything else.

Gina and her sister were gone.

Chapter 31

Charlie stood on the top step of Jennie's house—his house for the time being, at least technically—holding a nine-by-twelve manilla envelope in his hand. He toyed with the metal clasp holding it closed and waited for Jennie to come to the door.

He felt a lump in his throat when he heard the locks turn.

Jennie opened the door holding two bottles of beer in her hand. She handed one to Charlie and stepped outside, sat down on the top step and looked at his salt-stained boots.

She looked good, he thought.

She always did.

He took a sip of the beer she'd handed him and sat down next to her on the step. "Here," he said. He handed her the envelope.

She paused a moment before she took it, placed it down next to her without looking at the contents inside.

Charlie looked away, his eyes on the new picture window Jennie had replaced after the shooter blew out the old one. "They repair the inside walls yet?" he said.

Jennie nodded. "Looks better than it did before. Just wish someone could have saved that clock. I still remember my father taking it apart when I was little, got it working again after my aunt died."

"That clock was your aunt's?" he said. "I thought all this time it was your grandmother's?"

She looked at him but didn't answer.

Charlie took a sip of beer, resting his elbows on his knees. He looked out toward the street. "You sure you're gonna be okay?"

She leaned into him, shoulder to shoulder, gave him a friendly, maybe even flirting shove. She grinned. "I'm still going to worry about you, Charlie Harlow. But I'll sleep better at night not knowing when you're home in bed or out dodging bullets."

Charlie glanced back at her and grinned.

They both sat quiet.

"They cleared me," he said, still leaning forward but looking back at Jennie.

"I heard. It's good news, right?"

"You heard? From *who*?"

"Frank told me."

Charlie straightened up and turned his body to face her. "When did you talk with Frank?"

"He drove down last night after they'd captured Hunter King. Said he thought I'd like to know he was behind bars and I shouldn't have anything else to worry about."

"He knew I was cleared? Gunner pulled that trigger, Hunter—the older brother—admitted he took the gun from his brother's hands."

She took a sip of her beer and nodded. "That's what Frank told me."

Charlie scratched the back of his neck, looked out toward the street. "What else did he tell you?"

Jennie gave Charlie one of her looks, cracked a crooked smile and turned her eyes ahead. She sipped her beer, not saying another word about it.

Again, they sat quiet, the only sound coming from the tree frogs watching down at them for the evening.

"You still dating that teacher?" Charlie said. "Or whatever it is he does?"

"He's a professor," Jennie said.

"Oh. Same difference." He sipped his beer and just about finished the bottle without even realizing it.

She said, "We're just friends, Charlie."

He shrugged, trying to make like he didn't care. "You like him?"

She rolled her eyes. "You just signed those papers, Charlie. I'm not sure we need to talk about things like this just yet." She rested her hand on his back. "Maybe some other time we can be more open though." She smiled.

"Okay. But we're no longer Mr. and Mrs. Harlow. So we're both free to—"

"Charlie," she said. "Just stop asking questions like that. Okay?"

He huffed out a slight laugh, shaking his head, placed his empty bottle next to him on the concrete step and glanced at Jennie.

But she looked away. He leaned forward and tried to get a look into her eyes. He saw a tear coming down her cheek.

"Isn't this what you've wanted?" he said.

She sat, quiet.

"Jennie?" He stood up from the step and walked down the stairs, stood with his back to her and looked across at the neighbor's house. "Sometimes I don't understand you, Jennie." He turned back and they held each other's gaze.

Jennie wiped the tears from her cheeks. "It doesn't mean it's supposed to be easy." She smiled, her lips tight together. "Besides, I'm going to miss hounding you... calling you every day for the last eleven months... meeting you, trying to get you to sign those damn papers."

Charlie shrugged and forced a smile, feeling a little sad himself but not about to show it. "You can still take me out to lunch once in a while."

Jennie smiled, walked down the steps and leaned into Charlie, wrapping her arms around his neck. She rested her head on his shoulder. "I'll always love you, Charlie."

Just as he was about to say something sweet, his phone rang. *Shit*, he thought. He knew he had to answer it. "I'm sorry." He stepped back from her and looked at the screen. "It's Frank, I have to—"

"You don't have to explain, Charlie. Not anymore."

He turned from Jennie. "Frank?" He took a few steps along the walkway toward his Suburban parked in the driveway.

"I've been here waiting for you," Frank said. "I know you're with Jennie, but..."

"I'm on my way," Charlie said. He hung up without another word and turned to Jennie. "I'm sorry. I gotta run." He picked up his empty bottle from the top step, but Jennie took it from his hand. "Thanks for the beer," he said.

She put her foot on the bottom step and reached for the envelope on the top step where she'd been sitting. She held it in her hand and looked down at it. She played with the metal clasp like she was going to open it. But she didn't. "Goodbye, Charlie." She turned and walked up and into the house, closing the door behind her without looking back.

Charlie didn't move until he heard the lock snap inside the door. He stood there for another few seconds, maybe more. He finally turned, got back in the Suburban, and headed back to Asheville.

Ready for another thrilling adventure with Charlie Harlow? *Trackdown* is the second book in the series. Turn the page and enjoy the first three chapters from *Trackdown* or find out more by visiting PayetteStories.com

Chapter 1

Charlie could tell by the look on Lindsey's face, she'd had enough of the two young men down the other end of the bar.

Other than the two fools and the music down low on the jukebox, it was quiet at the Coyote Grille. The rough-sawn plank walls gave the long and narrow place the warm feel Charlie liked, on top of it being somewhat dark, other than the dim, canned lights hanging over the bar from the ceiling by cords. The only other light came from the streetlamp outside over the parking lot, shining through the windows at the backs of the two men.

There was a new country song playing that Charlie had never heard before. He didn't like the new stuff very much and preferred *traditional* country: songs by musicians who weren't even around anymore. He always said Johnny Cash made whiskey taste better.

A cool breeze came in through the door that Lindsey, the bartender, liked to leave open a crack. Feeling it at his back had him thinking how fast the summers went by, darkness setting in earlier with each passing day.

The Coyote Grille was up on the second level, with a deck outside the door overlooking the parking lot. It was above a couple of retail establishments down on the ground floor. One was a flower shop and the other some kind of music store that never seemed to be open. Charlie remembered an accountant or some kind of bookkeeper with an office down there, in the back, but never thought to see if he was still there.

Lindsey lived upstairs in the loft apartment over the bar, making it convenient when Charlie didn't feel like driving home. Or when she didn't want to be alone. She could handle herself, kept a 12-gauge behind the bar, but sometimes he worried about her when he wasn't there, especially with a couple of clowns like the two at the end of the bar, who had been drinking all day.

Charlie held his glass of Jack Daniels up in front of him, looking to his right out of the corner of his eye. He nudged his boss, Chief Deputy Frank Carter, as Lindsey told the two young men to finish up their beers, they'd had enough.

Jessie and Dustin didn't appear to like that very much.

Frank gave Charlie a look like he didn't want anything to do with it, sipped from his glass, and stared straight ahead. His voice low, he said, "Let's just hope they finish up and get out of here. I'm not in the mood for dealing with any small-town bullshit right now." He finished what was left in his glass and pushed it forward on the bar.

Charlie was familiar with Dustin and Jessie Redhouse, two brothers who had been in and out of the courthouse Charlie and Frank worked out of. He'd never personally had to deal with either of them, but Charlie knew when they were around, and there was booze involved, there was always a chance there'd be trouble.

He couldn't help but hear every word Dustin and Jessie were saying, their voices louder with each drink.

Dustin was the younger of the two. "She's gotta be out of high school," he said. "Sleeps out there by the fountain on the concrete bench." He laughed. "Got her own pool, can go in and skinny-dip whenever she wants."

Frank had said something, but Charlie's ears were locked on the two brothers, trying to piece together what they might've been talking about. He leaned toward Frank. "You hearin' any of this?"

Frank shook his head. "I told you, I don't want to have to deal with those two idiots. In fact, one more drink and I'm heading home, get my beauty rest."

Frank started to say something else, but Charlie put his hand on Frank's arm. "Shhh." He looked straight ahead toward the shelves of liquor on the back wall but listened with his good ear.

Dustin said, "I heard she puts on a bikini at night, goes in the fountain, picks out all the coins people tossed in. I bet she pulls twenty dollars a day."

Jessie, the older of the two, was almost twice the size of his skinny younger brother. He lifted his mug by the handle and guzzled what was left of his beer. "Twenty's a couple of good meals," he said, laughing. His face went serious, turning to Dustin. "She any good looking at all?"

Lindsey poured Frank another drink and pushed the glass toward him, looking at Charlie like she knew what he was thinking, his eyes focused on the two brothers. She had a worried look on her face and walked down the other end toward the two brothers, using her hands to lean on the bar in front of them. She said, "What's this I hear you two talkin' about?"

Dustin and Jessie both straightened out on their stools and looked up at Lindsey. They shrugged, shaking their heads.

"Nothin'," Jessie said.

"Well, I heard what you were saying, and it didn't sound like nothing. Something about a girl? Living outside?"

Dustin, the younger one, nodded. "She's living at the Fillmore Shopping Center, sleeps outside by the fountain, right there in front of that Mexican place."

Jessie elbowed his brother hard, like he wanted Dustin to keep his mouth shut.

"*What!*" Dustin said, rubbing his arm, looking at Jessie.

"You know who she is?" Lindsey said, peeking over her shoulder at Charlie and Frank, both watching her now.

Jessie and Dustin shook their heads.

Charlie leaned into Frank, his voice low. "I hope these two idiots don't think about driving over there, doing something stupid over at that shopping center. I don't like the idea, all those beers in 'em already, got their minds on a young woman who no doubt's vulnerable."

Frank's phone rang. He picked it up from the bar and looked at the screen, standing up from his stool. He said to Charlie, "I gotta take this one outside." He threw back his drink and turned for the door. "Order us one more, will you?" The door creaked as Frank opened it, then he pushed on the screen door and stepped outside.

The evening air was cool on Charlie's back, the door wide open now. He turned and looked through the screen at the moon shining over the tall pine trees surrounding the parking lot. Frank stood on the far end of the deck, his back to Charlie, leaning on the rail with the phone up to his ear.

Charlie got up and closed the interior door, leaving it open enough to keep the fresh air coming in. As he sat back down on his stool, he heard Lindsey tell the brothers they'd had enough.

She walked over to Charlie, the brothers watching her from behind like they'd never seen a woman's backside before.

Charlie lifted his glass and cleared his throat loud enough for the two to hear. "Let's show a little respect, all right?"

"I can handle myself," Lindsey said, keeping her voice quiet. She picked up Frank's glass. "He stick you with the tab again?"

Charlie smiled, shaking his head. "He's outside on a call." He finished his drink and placed the empty glass in front of him.

Lindsey grabbed the bottle of Jack Daniels from the shelf behind her and filled both Charlie's and Frank's glasses.

Dustin, the younger brother with the big mouth, slapped his hand down on the bar. "Hey, if you're still pouring for them, then why can't we have no more?"

Jessie said, "Come on, Lindsey, give us one more."

Lindsey rolled her eyes and looked at Charlie, acting as if she hadn't heard them.

"Hey!" Jessie yelled. "You hear me?"

Lindsey had a look like she knew she'd already made a mistake giving the brothers one beer too many.

"How about a couple sodas?" she said, picking up a bottle from the shelf, wiping it down with a towel.

"We don't want no goddamn sodas," Dustin said, pushing up his sleeves, showing off the tattoos running up and down each arm.

Charlie glanced toward the door, wondering if Frank would be on his way back inside. He didn't like where things were going, both Redhouse brothers not as bad as some of the others until too much liquor flowed through their blood.

For Charlie, having a drink or three was a way to relax after a hard day's work, knowing the next day would be harder if he had too much. And as much as he liked the Coyote Grille and the pretty proprietor behind the bar, he didn't like the almost weekly occurrence of having to deal with a fool who couldn't handle his liquor.

Charlie had asked her more than once if she'd ever consider selling the place. He'd said to her at one point, "What about hiring a full-time bouncer?" But she couldn't afford to do either, she'd said to Charlie. Not unless a rich man came in and swept her off her feet so she didn't have to work another day in her life.

But the truth was, she could take care of herself with the Mossberg twelve gauge she kept behind the bar and a Smith & Wesson .38 tucked behind the register. Growing up in Weaverville, on the northern edge of Asheville, Lindsey knew most of the people who walked into her bar. That included not only the Redhouse brothers, but their now deceased father, who used to sit on the same end of the bar as his sons.

Charlie didn't know much about their upbringing, other than they'd been raised by their mother after the father had been killed holding up a convenience store out in Marshall, just east of Weaverville.

"Can't we please just have one more?" Jessie said. "We ain't driving." He'd tried to change his tone, like a child begging for a cookie, but Charlie wasn't buying.

Lindsey grabbed the broom and started sweeping behind the bar. "I've learned my lesson with you boys," she said.

Dustin grabbed his empty mug and turned in his stool, raising the mug over his head and tossing it behind him. The glass smashed against the wall on a painting between the two windows and shattered into pieces.

Charlie was on his feet and down the other end of the bar before Dustin had a chance to turn around in his seat, ripping him from the stool by his shirt. He pinned him on the floor without much effort and pressed his knee down onto his chest.

But Jessie was up from his seat and grabbed Charlie from behind, had his arms wrapped around Charlie's neck, trying to wrestle him off his brother.

Charlie held on to Dustin with one hand, had his shirt bunched up in his closed fist, and threw a quick elbow behind him, catching Jessie square in the mouth.

Jessie went crashing into the table behind them and tipped it over as he fell to the floor. He got up on his feet, holding his face with one hand; blood dripping from his mouth through his fingers. He ran for the door and took off outside, leaving his brother behind. The screen door slammed closed behind him.

Lindsey yelled for Charlie to let him go, coming around the bar with the broom still in her hand.

Charlie looked up at her, wondered if she was going to hit him with the handle but eased up his grasp on Dustin's shirt.

Dustin got up, stumbling, nearly tripping over himself trying to get out of there. He brushed past Lindsey, almost knocking her back as he ran for the door after his big brother.

"Goddamnit," Lindsey said, looking down at all the broken glass. She grabbed the tab she'd left for them and turned, holding it up for Charlie as he lifted the table from the floor. She said, "You could've at least waited until they paid their tab."

The door opened, and Frank walked in, looking behind him toward the outside. "What the hell'd you do now?" he said, eyes on Charlie.

Charlie picked his hat off the floor and didn't answer, brushing the dust off the bill. He looked at his hand, feeling something sharp, like he might've had a piece of glass stuck in it. He picked at his finger, removed a tiny shard sticking out from it. Placing his hat back on his head, he gave Frank a nod. "Dustin dropped his mug."

Frank looked down at the hardwoods as Charlie crouched down with a dustpan to help Lindsey sweeping up the broken mug.

She took the dustpan from Charlie and started back to the other side of the bar. "You two go on over and finish up," she said, looking toward the clock behind the bar. "I'm closing early." She walked around the bar with the broom in one hand and the dustpan filled with glass in the other, disappearing through the swinging door and into the back.

Charlie and Frank went over and sat down again, and Frank said, "I don't understand why she keeps letting those boys back in."

Charlie picked up his glass, held it in front of his chin. "She wouldn't have any customers; she kicked out all the ones who caused trouble."

Charlie walked a few steps behind Frank across the parking lot, looked up at the full moon coming over the trees. He zipped his jacket and said, "Cold feels like it's coming in early this year. I'm not sure I'm ready for it. Not that I like all that heat this summer much, either."

Frank headed for his car without much else to say but stopped and turned when Charlie said his name.

"I was thinking," Charlie said. "You think one of us should drive by Fillmore Shopping Center?"

Frank appeared to be thinking it over, then looked at his watch. "What are you looking to accomplish? Smartest thing might be, call the local police."

Charlie looked over toward the Suburban he'd been driving. "I've gotta drive down and see Jennie."

"This late?" Frank said.

Charlie nodded. "Was supposed to be there a half hour ago. Something about hiring someone to fix the railing on the front steps."

"You can't fix it yourself?" Frank had a funny look on his face, like he was holding back a grin.

"Well, what I should do is remind her it's not my house anymore. But either way, she said someone'll fall, break their neck by the time I got around to fixing it myself."

Frank opened the driver's-side door of his blue Ford F-150, resting one foot up on the running board. "I have to go by the office, check on a few things. I can swing by the shopping center, if it'll help you sleep tonight."

Charlie thought for a moment. "You know what? I'll go there now. It's on my way out to see Jennie." He started to turn from Frank but stopped. "I just don't like the idea of those Redhouse boys, having a young girl on their minds in there, all those drinks they had inside 'em."

Frank stepped up into his truck, leaned out with his hand on the door's inside handle. "Like I said, probably something for the locals to contend with. But I know sometimes you just can't help yourself." Frank closed the door and started the engine. He drove off without another word, tires crunching on the broken asphalt.

Charlie watched the taillights on Frank's truck disappear beyond the trees and turned for his Suburban. Under his breath, even though Frank was gone, he said, "See you in the morning, boss."

Chapter 2

CHARLIE WALKED ACROSS ONE of the parking lots at the Fillmore Shopping Center, having a hard time remembering the last time he'd been there. It was more run-down at the time with half the stores gone. But it looked like a different place, all new with mostly national chains, like you see in just about any shopping center in Anytown, USA.

The fountain was still there, and he remembered it well, back when he and Jennie used to go a couple times a week for lunch when they were married. But the restaurant they used to order from looked to be gone, replaced with yet another take-out restaurant chain. He had a friend who had been in the restaurant business, but had gotten out with the high rents only the chains could afford. It was why Charlie would drive a little out of his way to get a drink or a sandwich at the Coyote Grille. Other than, of course, to see Lindsey. A good hole-in-the-wall that would stick around for a couple of generations was hard to come by.

He walked over the wood-plank bridge crossing over what looked to be a man-made brook and looked past the empty black tables with open umbrellas. There were a few people eating at a roped-off patio at a place called Four Brothers Burgers, which Charlie thought might've been owned by some Hollywood actor and his siblings, but couldn't remember which.

He walked past a stage with a sign that said LIVE MUSIC EVERY FRIDAY NIGHT THROUGH THE LAST WEEKEND IN SEPTEMBER.

But it was already October.

The sound from the fountain's jets shooting water into the air grew louder as he approached the far end of the outdoor area, the water glistening in the colored lights pointed up toward the dark sky. He liked the peaceful sounds of the fountain, but it still felt artificial, as did everything else around him.

His phone rang, and he removed it from his pocket. When he saw it was Jennie, he knew it wouldn't be good. He should have been there already. "Hey, Jennie," he said, answering.

"Charlie?" she said, her voice raised. "What the hell is wrong with you? I asked you to be here an hour ago. The contractor's on his way now."

"You asked, but I told you I wouldn't be able to get there that soon. I had some work to do."

Although it was late, there were a handful of kids running around, the parents watching but not paying much attention. As much as Charlie despised his father for most of his life, he was glad he took him out to the mountains and taught him the beauty of nature instead of dragging him to a fountain at a shopping center because it was convenient.

Jennie was yapping in Charlie's ear, but he was only half listening, looking for a young woman who may appear to be homeless, whatever that would even look like.

"Did you hear me?" Jennie said.

And all Charlie could do was be honest. "No, not really. You're yelling."

"I'm not yelling," she said. "You said you'd help me with this railing."

"It's just a railing, Jennie. Not that big a deal."

"So you're not coming?"

"Yes, I'm coming. I just had to make a quick stop." He looked at his watch. "Should be there in ten, fifteen minutes." Of course, he knew it would take him at least twenty to get to Hendersonville, if he drove fast enough. "I'm sorry, Jennie. I'm looking for a girl. A young woman."

"I told you already, what you do with your personal life is none of my business anymore."

"Not like that," he said. "I'm at the Fillmore Shopping Center. By the fountain where we used to come eat."

"Oh," she said, but that was it. The line was quiet for a moment.

"I'll see you soon. I'm sorry to keep you waiting." He hung up the phone without giving her a chance to say another word, tucked his phone in his pocket, and sat on the concrete edge of the fountain, tucking his boots in underneath him so he didn't trip one of the kids running by. He looked all around but didn't see a girl who might fit what he had in mind. It was mostly couples, looking like kids themselves, with their young kids.

A man just a few feet away helped a young boy stand on top of the fountain's edge and toss pennies in.

There was no sign of the girl. And no sign of Dustin or Jessie, either.

Charlie looked at the time on his phone and headed for the parking lot, dialing his phone to call Frank as he walked back to his vehicle. "I'm leaving the shopping center right now," he said. "No girl here that I could find."

"You see the brothers?" Frank said.

"No. Nothing."

Frank was quiet on the other end. "I left Chief Brayden a message to call me, let him know about her. I'm not sure there's much any of us'll be able to do." He paused on the other end. "Charlie, I'm sure someone out there appreciates your concern. But you also have to remember the source. We have no way of knowing for sure the story those two clowns were spouting holds any truth."

Charlie pointed his key fob at the Suburban and unlocked the doors, stepping up inside. "I thought about that," he said. "Or maybe she's gone home."

Charlie made it down to Jennie's house—*his* house, before they divorced—in just under twenty minutes, on top of the ten he'd spent looking around the shopping center before he left.

He turned in the driveway but had to back out when a truck parked behind Jennie's car had the reverse lights on. Charlie waited in the street in front of the house, gave the man in the truck a nod as he drove past him, then pulled back into the driveway.

Jennie was in the doorway watching Charlie, and he could see it in her face. *She's in one of her moods,* he thought. He walked over the brick walkway toward the front door.

"You're unbelievable," she said, looking out through the screen. "You promised me you'd be here to meet the contractor."

Charlie shook his head. "I told you I could be here, just not as soon as you wanted me to be." Charlie looked back at the red lights on the rear of the contractor's truck as it disappeared down the road. "Why's he coming out so late? When it's dark out?"

Jennie pushed open the door and held it open. "I assume he's on the job all day." She just about let it close on him and turned from the door as he reached for the handle.

Charlie stepped inside. "It's just a railing," he said. "Can't imagine there's much involved in fixing it." He looked around the living room just inside to his left. The furniture was different. He could smell it: brand-new furniture and whatever chemicals they spray on them. "What'd you do with my old couch?"

"Got rid of it."

"*Got rid of it?*" he said. "It was brand new."

Jennie laughed, stepping out from the kitchen with a glass of red wine in one hand, a cut carrot in her other. She took a bite of the carrot, using it to point into the living room area with the new furniture. "We've had that couch since we first got married, Charlie. It was time for it to go. And besides, it didn't match the new paint."

Charlie looked at the walls and hadn't even noticed the new off-white color, when he first walked in. "I would've taken it, if you'd told me you were getting rid of it."

"And do *what* with it?" she said. "I don't think it'd even fit in that trailer you're living in now."

"It's a Winnebago," he said.

Jennie walked back into the kitchen and opened the refrigerator, her back to Charlie. "You want a beer?"

He said, "Does this mean you're not mad?"

She took out a bottle of Yuengling and opened the top, handing it to him. She threw the cap in the garbage under the sink and poured more wine into her glass. "I just wish you'd keep your word," she said. "That's all."

Charlie didn't even bother trying to explain. He'd made it clear he couldn't be there when she wanted him to. It was a losing battle with Jennie, no matter what. It was different when they were first married, happy for those first bunch of years. But then it just turned into, no matter what he said, him being the one who was wrong. Always. Even though they were divorced, it hadn't changed much at all. If he said something was black, she'd say it was white.

"You're the one who keeps telling me not to let anyone in here I don't know, without you being around. What was I supposed to tell that man? You'll have to come back, my ex-husband's not here?"

Charlie sipped his beer. "I told you on the phone, I went by the Fillmore Shopping Center to check on a girl—a young woman—supposedly living there, outside. I don't know what the story is. But she wasn't there, so maybe she's not anymore."

"Isn't that something for the police to deal with?"

Charlie nodded. "It is, normally. But I was at the Coyote Grille and—"

"The Coyote Grille?" Jennie huffed. "You said you were working late, not going to your girlfriend's bar."

Charlie cracked a small smile. He couldn't help but like when Jennie got jealous, even though he never wanted Jennie to find out about Lindsey in the first place.

"I met Frank. But if you'd let me finish..."

Jennie looked back at him, sipping her wine.

He said, "There are these two brothers who were there. Been in and out of trouble since they were kids. And when they started talking about this young woman they'd heard had been sleeping at the shopping center by the fountain, I just thought..."

Jennie said, "You think they'd go over there? Cause trouble?"

"Wouldn't put it past either of them," Charlie said. "You know, if something were to happen to her and I didn't at least make some kind of effort to make sure she was all right..."

Jennie held her wineglass up in front of her mouth, a look on her face like she was trying to cover up a smile.

"Did I say something funny?" Charlie said, staring back at her.

"No, not at all. I'm sorry."

"Then what's that smirk on your face?"

She looked toward the floor, then raised her gaze to Charlie. "You're a good guy, Charlie Harlow."

He said, "If you think so highly of me, why'd we divorce?"

Jennie rolled her eyes. "Can't I just say something nice about you without having to go down this road every time?" She turned and started back into the kitchen.

Charlie looked her over from behind. "You still look the way you did when we were married, you know."

"You mean, from behind?" She turned and looked back over her shoulder, down at herself.

Charlie laughed.

Jennie picked up a yellow sheet of paper off the counter. "Here's the quote for the work on the steps."

Charlie reached out and took it from her, looking it over with his eyes open wide. "Is he serious? This much? To fix a railing?"

She shook her head. "I told you already, if you'd only listen. It's not just the railing. He has to re-cement the steps... or whatever you call it."

Charlie wasn't sure. Re-cement sounded about right. He'd worked construction when he was younger, before he decided to join the Marshals Service, but it was never really his thing.

"So what are you going to do about the girl?" she said. "Is she okay?"

Charlie raised his eyes from the paper and put it back down on the counter. He thought for a moment, then shrugged. "Frank already left a message with Asheville PD. Chief Brayden. Hopefully, they won't just brush it off."

Chapter 3

It was early morning when Charlie poured himself a coffee and stepped out the door of his Winnebago, parked on the edge of the Swannanoa River. Steam rose from his cup in the cold air as Charlie took a sip, watching the sun creeping up in the distance through the trees. The property was owned by a friend of Charlie's who'd said he could stay there as long as he liked. He told Charlie he planned to build a house there one day but wasn't sure he'd ever get to it.

Charlie had gotten the 1983 Winnebago from the auction, but at the time had no idea it would one day become his home. It was only after his divorce from Jennie was final, he decided he didn't need a house. And he couldn't see living in one of those new apartments with all those people crammed together in one building.

He sat down on a picnic table with his coffee, staring out at the river. A flock of birds flew high in formation, and Charlie thought, with the early chill, they were heading south. He kept his eyes on the birds until they disappeared beyond the trees. He never minded the cold and remembered Jennie saying one day they should retire to Florida.

Not his thing, he told her.

He sat, quiet, enjoying the fresh air and quiet all around him. He hadn't been able to get the girl, sleeping at the shopping center, off his mind, and started to wonder if he'd looked hard enough. He should've gone back after he left Jennie's.

What if the brothers showed up when she was there, after the crowd had gone?

The Fillmore Shopping Center was empty and quiet, other than the sound of a single-engine plane flying high over Charlie's head.

He walked toward the fountain and over the wooden footbridge, from the parking lot, the sounds of the fountain growing louder as it covered over the quiet. The sun was up high enough now, he could see the water from the fountain sparkle in the morning sun's rays. He sipped the coffee he'd picked up on the drive out—as if he hadn't had enough caffeine already—and looked back and forth at the closed shops and restaurants on either side of where he walked. Everything looked to be at least a couple of hours from opening.

He didn't see any sign of the girl. At least not until he stepped closer to the fountain and looked across, through the jets of water, and saw someone lying flat on a bench, covered with a blanket. He walked closer and saw long, dark hair coming out from under it, hanging down.

He waited, watching for movement before he went around to the other side of the fountain. He didn't want to startle her, although he could only assume it was the girl he'd gone there looking for.

As he stepped closer, he wasn't exactly sure what he would say or how she would react to a stranger walking up to her, asleep on a bench in a shopping center well before seven in the morning.

Even with the bright sun coming out of the blue sky, the air had a pretty good chill to it. With October right around the corner, he couldn't imagine how she could continue sleeping outside.

Charlie stood over her and removed his sunglasses, squinting as he reached down and tapped her on the shoulder. "Hey, are you okay?"

The girl's eyes sprang open, and she jumped into a seated position, her feet up on the bench. She tucked her legs close to her chest with her arms wrapped around her knees, holding them against her. "Who the hell are you?" she said, looking up at him.

Charlie had his badge ready in his hand. "Deputy U.S. Marshal Charlie Harlow. I'm here to… I just want to make sure you're all right. I'm not going to hurt you."

She didn't respond at first, staring back at him like she'd just come out of a deep sleep, looking around the fountain as if she was getting ready to run.

Charlie was surprised how young she looked. Younger than he'd expected. She really was just a kid. "Like I said, I'm just checking to make sure you're okay." He looked past her at the wooded area between where they stood and the parking lot on the other side, fifty yards away. "I'm just not sure this is a safe place for a young lady to be sleeping out here, all alone."

She swallowed, nodding. "I'm… I'm fine."

Charlie said, "What's your name?"

"Are you really a marshal?"

He nodded.

"Do you stop terrorists from hijacking planes?"

Charlie smiled. He'd heard that one at least a few dozen times before. "That's the US Air Marshals." He pointed to the emblem on the chest of his jacket. "U.S. Marshals Service. I don't even like to fly."

"So, like the police?"

"No, not really."

"Not really?"

He paused, smiling again at the young girl's inquisitive nature. She seemed confident enough, less worried about living outside on a bench than most people might be. "You going to tell me your name?"

"Haley."

"You have a last name, Haley?"

"Am I in trouble?"

He shook his head. "Not at all, Haley. I told you already, I was just checking up on you."

She squinted her eyes, reached into a plastic GAP bag under the bench and took out a pair of sunglasses. The bag looked to be stuffed with clothes. "Haley Moore," she said, looking up at Charlie. She put her feet down on the concrete and folded up the blanket.

Charlie lifted his sunglasses from his pocket and slipped them over his eyes. He looked around and through the fountain's jets, seeing someone walking into one of the shops, assuming it was a person who worked there, opening up for the day. "Listen, so how long've you been sleeping out here like this?"

She shrugged. "I don't know. Three weeks, I guess?"

"Three weeks? You've been living out here like this for three weeks? That's a long time, isn't it? And nobody's bothered you?"

She shrugged again. "People are nice around here, for the most part." She held up the folded blanket. "Some lady came by and gave me this a few nights ago, when the temperature dropped."

"You don't have anywhere else you can stay? Relatives? Parents? Something happen to them?"

She looked down toward the ground. "Just my dad. But we don't get along."

"No?" Charlie almost wanted to tell her he knew first-hand what she meant but didn't go into it. He waited, thinking maybe she'd offer more. "So you're dad's all right with you out here all by yourself, sleeping on a bench?"

She didn't respond, looking straight ahead now toward the fountain's water spraying high into the air.

And Charlie didn't want to push, make her say anything more than she was comfortable saying. He noticed a bottle of ketchup under the bench and wondered if that might've been her dinner. "You want something to eat?"

She looked at him, shaking her head. "No, I'm good."

"You're good?" he said. "It doesn't look like you're good." He grinned. "Just being honest with you, Haley."

She let out a crooked smile, bouncing her heel off the concrete.

"How about I go get you some food, huh? Bring it back so you have something to eat for breakfast?"

A slight breeze came across the area, blowing Haley's hair down over her sunglasses. She pushed it back and used her sunglasses to keep it in place on top of her head. With her eyes squinted, she looked up at Charlie. "I'm okay."

He wasn't buying it. "I'm sure you are. But you need to eat. I'm just offering to grab you something. We don't have to make a big deal about it, all right?"

She slipped her sunglasses back down over her eyes.

"You eat eggs? Bagels?"

With a shrug, she nodded again. "Sure."

"I bet a hot coffee would do you all right, too, huh?"

She smiled this time. "Thanks."

"Will you be right here when I get back?"

"I don't have anywhere else to go just yet."

Charlie's phone rang in his pocket as he walked out from Benny's Bagel Shop on the other side of the shopping center, a bag with two bagel sandwiches in one hand and a tray with a coffee and a clear plastic bottle of orange juice in the other. He walked across the street to where he'd parked the Suburban and put the bag on the hood, but was too late by the time he'd taken his phone out to answer.

But as soon as he saw it was Kim—Deputy U.S. Marshal Kim Riggins—he tapped the screen and returned her call without waiting to see if she'd left a message. "You looking for me?" he said as soon as she answered.

"Frank is. He asked me to call, see if you were coming to the office."

Charlie unlocked the driver's-side door and opened it, placing the cardboard tray on top of the center console. "Why wouldn't I be coming in?" He stepped around the door and grabbed the bag off the hood.

"I'm not exactly sure. He's in one of his moods, forgets I'm not his secretary. Sounds like he's got something for you: failure to appear, down in Hendersonville. I think he may've hoped you were still down at your house."

"Well, it's not my house anymore. And I wouldn't be down there." He stepped into the Suburban and slid the key into the ignition. "I'm ten minutes from the office. You think he wants me to go down there?"

Kim sighed into the phone. "You're asking questions you know I can't answer. Between the two of you..."

Charlie laughed. "Tell him I'll give him a call as soon as I'm done."

"Done with *what*? I have to tell him something."

"Uh, I'm at the Fillmore Shopping Center. Just gotta take care of something."

"This have something to do with the young woman sleeping over there, on the bench?"

"Frank told you? I'm not even sure I'd call her a young woman. She's a kid. A girl."

Charlie had already jumped back on 26 and took the first exit, not even a quarter mile away, onto Fillmore Parkway. He drove into the shopping center lot closest to the fountain, parking the Suburban in a space to the left of the footbridge.

"You know how old she is?" Kim said.

"I don't. I'd be surprised she's even eighteen, nineteen maybe."

"Well, that's not a little girl, Charlie."

He stepped out and tucked the bag with the two sandwiches under his arm, held the phone with his shoulder, carried the tray in one hand, and grabbed his phone with the other.

Kim said, "Did you find her?"

"Yeah, I actually talked to her. She didn't say much, but I'm bringing her something to eat right now." He walked over the bridge and saw a man with a long pole down across the courtyard, standing on the edge of the fountain. The water jets were turned off, and the man appeared to be doing some work to it or maybe just cleaning it out.

Charlie was too far away to be sure, but when he looked through the jets of water, he didn't see Haley on the other side. "Kim, let me call you back, all right?"

"What do you want me to tell Frank?" she said.

"I don't know. Give me a few minutes. I'll call you right back." He hung up without another word, walked around the fountain to the empty bench. He looked around, wondering where she could've gone and why she didn't wait for him, like she said she would.

He went back around to the other side where the man had a long pole with a net on the other end, skimming leaves and debris from the top of the fountain's pool. Charlie approached him. "Morning."

The man turned and gave him a nod. "Good morning."

Charlie said, "You happen to see a girl, a young lady, over there on that bench? Was here maybe about fifteen minutes ago?"

The man nodded. "Of course. She's here all the time." He looked Charlie over. "Who are *you*?"

Charlie held up the white bag, holding the tray in his other hand. "Just brought her some breakfast." He didn't pull his badge. He didn't think he needed to, not when he wasn't technically acting under any kind of official business. "Any chance you know where she might've gone?"

The man shook his head, removed the skimmer from the water and emptied whatever was inside it with his hands, into a bucket next to him. "I don't usually see her around during the day. She's here early in the morning but usually disappears once people start showing up. At least until later in the evening."

Charlie put the bag and tray on top of the fountain's edge. "If you see her, would you mind making sure she gets this?"

The man looked down at the food and drinks, nodding. "Sure thing."

"Thank you," Charlie said. He started to walk away and stopped, turning back to the man. "She don't show up, go ahead and help yourself. Hate to see it all go to waste."

See below for more books by Gregory Payette or visit
PayetteStories.com

JAKE HORN MYSTERIES
A Ring and a Prayer (Series prequel)
A Good Time for Goodbye
The Silence of the Sand
When the Smoke Clears

HENRY WALSH MYSTERIES
Dead at Third
The Last Ride
The Crystal Pelican
The Night the Music Died
Dead Men Don't Smile
Dead in the Creek
Dropped Dead
Dead Luck
A Shot in the Dark
Dead or a Lie

JOE SHELDON SERIES
Play It Cool
Play It Again
Play It Down

U.S. MARSHAL CHARLIE HARLOW
Shake the Trees
Trackdown
Half Moon Rising

GREGORY PAYETTE

CRIME FICTION/STANDALONES
Biscayne Boogie
Tell Them I'm Dead
Drag the Man Down
Half Cocked
Danny Womack's .38

www.ingramcontent.com/pod-product-compliance
Ingram Content Group UK Ltd.
Pitfield, Milton Keynes, MK11 3LW, UK
UKHW041301180426
11947UKWH00009B/597

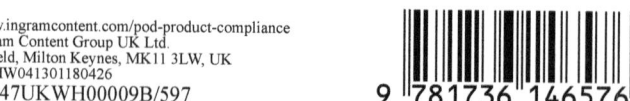